"Sweetheart," Castor said coolly. "You shouldn't be here."

Glory gazed at him warily, as if he was a rabid dog who might attack at any moment. "I—I—I know. I wasn't invited." Her voice was low, husky and sent the most disturbing shiver of sexual awareness down his spine.

How inconvenient.

"No, of course you weren't invited. I know everyone on that guest list, and you weren't on it. So tell me, who are you and what the hell are you doing in my house?"

She stared at him for a moment, then squared her shoulders as if bracing herself for a distasteful task and took a step toward him.

"Actually," she said, "I'm here to make you an offer."

It wasn't unusual. Lots of people made him offers.

Castor raised an eyebrow. "You gate-crashed my party to make me an offer? What kind of offer?"

"I'd like to offer you..." She lifted her chin as if she was facing down a firing squad, then dramatically threw off her cloak. "My virginity."

Jackie Ashenden writes dark, emotional stories with alpha heroes who've just gotten the world to their liking only to have it blown apart by their kick-ass heroines. She lives in Auckland, New Zealand, with her husband, the inimitable Dr. Jax, two kids and two rats. When she's not torturing alpha males and their gutsy heroines, she can be found drinking chocolate martinis, reading anything she can lay her hands on, wasting time on social media or being forced to go mountain biking with her husband. To keep up-to-date with Jackie's new releases and other news, sign up to her newsletter at jackieashenden.com.

Books by Jackie Ashenden

Harlequin Presents

The Italian's Final Redemption
The World's Most Notorious Greek
The Innocent Carrying His Legacy
The Wedding Night They Never Had

Pregnant Princesses

Pregnant by the Wrong Prince

The Royal House of Axios

Promoted to His Princess
The Most Powerful of Kings

Visit the Author Profile page
at Harlequin.com for more titles.

Jackie Ashenden

THE INNOCENT'S ONE-NIGHT PROPOSAL

ISBN-13: 978-1-335-56847-2

The Innocent's One-Night Proposal

Harlequin Enterprises ULC
22 Adelaide St. West, 41st Floor
Toronto, Ontario M5H 4E3, Canada
www.Harlequin.com

Printed in U.S.A.

THE INNOCENT'S
ONE-NIGHT PROPOSAL

To Jo, Ayesha, latte bowls, flat whites, espressos and grabbing the last savory scone!

CHAPTER ONE

GLORY ALBRIGHT THOUGHT she might be in trouble when the first naked woman sauntered past her.

When a second followed, Glory realised she was totally out of her depth.

So. It appeared the rumours about how wild the parties at Castor Xenakis's Malibu mansion got were true.

Wild didn't even begin to cover it.

She pulled the cloak she wore tighter around her shoulders and concentrated very hard on the bookshelf in front of her rather than what was happening around her. There was a small sculpture sitting on one of the shelves. It was of a woman being embraced by a man and was carved out of white marble. The man had his hands…

Oh.

Glory blushed as she suddenly realised what kind of sculpture it was and wished she could turn around and find something else to look at, but since turning around might mean potentially seeing more naked people, the statue was clearly the lesser of the two evils.

This was a stupid idea. She shouldn't have come.

In the room at her back, she could hear people laughing and talking and shrieking. Music throbbed like a heartbeat. From elsewhere came the sounds of smashing glass and yet more loud laughter. Then a splash from the pool area.

Someone brushed against her as they walked past where she stood near the bookshelf, and she shrank away in discomfort.

Infamous parties/orgies at luxury Malibu beach houses were so far out of her comfort zone that she may as well have been on the moon, and if she'd had any choice in the matter she'd still be safely at home in the run-down apartment she shared with her sister, curled up in front of the TV watching reruns of *Friends* and eating ice cream.

But she didn't have a choice. Okay, perhaps that wasn't exactly true. She didn't *have* to decide she wanted to pay for her sister to have IVF treatment. And the plan she'd come up with didn't *need* to include gatecrashing the party of one of the most notorious playboys in the world. Neither did it *have* to involve her virginity, and selling said virginity to said playboy.

Then again, Annabel couldn't afford IVF and after the sacrifices she'd made in bringing Glory up after their parents' deaths, Glory thought helping her achieve her dream of having a family was a small price to pay.

Yes, the idea of selling her virginity to an infamous playboy might be a bit wild and wild wasn't Glory at all, but how else could she get a lot of money in a short space of time, and legally?

And this *was* Castor Xenakis after all. She hadn't spent months looking at the pictures of him in the gossip magazines for absolutely no reason. He might be a very bad man and she might tell herself she was doing this for Annabel's benefit, but the deeper truth beneath that was that she wanted him.

Those pictures had led to an obsession with him that she couldn't deny. An obsession that she was tired of and was hoping a night in his bed would cure her of.

Anyway, it wasn't as if she'd just dreamed her plan up on the fly. It had come to her after months spent reading said magazines at her job behind the counter of Mr and Mrs Jessup's grocery store, and then paying quiet attention to the customers who visited the store. Customers who talked. Customers who let slip certain things…

The plan was utter madness, of course, and totally alien to Glory's quiet nature, but when you were a dirt-poor checkout girl and your beloved older sister had given up a lot of dreams for you, then you did what you could to give those dreams back to her.

Exactly. And you didn't come here to stand in front of the bookshelf staring at naughty statues.

No, she hadn't.

She'd come to one of Castor Xenakis's notorious Malibu parties to find the world's most debauched and dissolute playboy himself, then offer him her virginity.

For a price.

It wasn't totally out of the realms of possibility that he'd accept. She had, after all, read *a lot* about him in those magazines that stood on a stand near the counter, because he was in those magazines constantly. And if the rumours about his parties were true, then she might have a chance.

He was supposed to choose a woman for the night from amongst the partygoers and whichever woman he chose apparently didn't go away empty-handed the next day. Money, jewellery, expensive purses were some of the gifts he gave to his lovers. One was even rumoured to have been given some expensive sports car.

Glory had been in the middle of reading one of those gossipy articles when a couple of women had come in, chattering about all the work they had to do for the party coming up that weekend.

She had sat there quietly, not drawing attention to herself, which she was very good at, just listening. Being able to fade into the background was a useful skill, since if people didn't notice you, they'd talk about all kinds of stuff.

Such as how the party was going to be a big one and how the boss himself was going to be there, and how he did like everything to go smoothly.

The two women were regulars and Glory knew they worked at Castor Xenakis's Malibu beach house, so he must have been the boss they were talking about.

Castor Xenakis, CEO of CX Enterprises—a multinational with interests in finance, shipping, construction and various other industries—and party circuit regular, had been linked to all kinds of scandals and was reputedly one of the most infamous womanisers in the western world, if not the entire globe.

The one who made extravagant gifts to his lovers.

It was then that her idea was born. Her mad, wild and very un-Glory-like idea.

There was no guarantee he'd accept her offer, and why would he when he had a legion of A-list Hollywood stars, supermodels and even royalty at his beck and call? Then again, he might be in the market for novelty, for something different, and Glory could safely say that she *was* different. At least for him. She wasn't beautiful, but she'd been told on a number of occasions—or at least shouted at by men—that she had a great body. But mainly, she was a total virgin. She hadn't even been kissed before. Men got off on that, or so she'd heard, and she was hoping Castor Xenakis would get off on it.

And if he doesn't, Annabel won't get a chance at having a baby.

That was true. And she wouldn't get her chance at a night with him either, which was disappointing.

She had to be rid of this obsession. How would she ever find someone in her own league if she kept thinking about a man normally so far beyond her reach he might as well have been on the moon?

Whatever, standing here feeling sick with nerves wasn't going to help with either of those two things.

First, she had to find him.

Steeling herself, Glory turned around.

The room was huge, running the entire width of the house. One wall was entirely floor-to-ceiling windows that faced the beach. Low, white leather modular couches were scattered everywhere, along with low glass tables, and sleek bookshelves devoid of actual books. Huge artworks—mostly abstract— adorned the white walls, and a number of other sculptural artworks stood on tables or on the white carpet of the floor.

The effect was one of stark luxury but Glory, who was fond of clutter, found it rather soulless.

People were scattered around the room, the women dressed in couture cocktail dresses and statement jewellery, the men in designer suits. She thought she might recognise some of the guests since it was definitely a place for the rich and famous, but so far she hadn't.

There were still laughter and lots of conversation, the music thumping, but she could see that there was a couple in the corner who were...

Oh. Right.

Glory moved quickly out of the room, her heart beating very fast, and into the soaring atrium-style entranceway. Massive globes of frosted glass hung suspended from the ceiling, looking like planets floating in space.

There were also people out here, though mostly clothed, thank God.

Glory wished she had the courage to ask one of them where Castor Xenakis was, but she didn't want to draw attention to herself. They might realise she hadn't been invited—she'd snuck in with a group of people dressed in burlesque costumes—and might decide to have her kicked out since it was clear she didn't belong here.

And she really didn't. The nudity, the alcohol, the luxury setting, the crowds of people and the uninhibited atmosphere were all making her extremely uncomfortable. She didn't do parties, never had, not even as a teenager. She'd been too busy taking care of Annabel after her breast cancer diagnosis, and there hadn't been time for any of that kind of thing even if she'd wanted to.

Not that she wanted to. Her life was quiet and steady and predictable, and that's just how she preferred it.

Which makes being here a really dumb idea.

Probably. But that IVF wasn't going to pay for itself and she was here now, and so she at least had to try.

Skirting a group of sketchy-looking men who were talking seriously and radiating 'do not disturb' vibes, Glory found another long hallway and started down it.

Perhaps Xenakis had withdrawn from the main

party and was in another room. He could be outside, of course, somewhere in the lush, tropical-style garden that surrounded the house, but she wanted to make sure he wasn't inside first before she braved whatever was going on outside.

Or perhaps she'd missed him? But no, he wasn't like her. He wasn't a man who would ever fade into the background and remain unnoticed.

Castor Xenakis couldn't remain unnoticed even if he tried.

He was phenomenally handsome and even in the photos Glory had pored over she'd been able to tell that he possessed the kind of charisma that drew people to him, that commanded attention simply by its very existence.

And you're hoping a man like that will choose you for the night? Are you actually insane?

Maybe. But as she'd sat reading about him in that magazine and then heard his two staff members chatting about the upcoming party, well…it had seemed like fate.

The throb of the party music was a little less down this corridor, but was now joined by the sound of a piano, which was odd.

She followed the sound, the notes cascading through the hallway, echoing off the hardwood floors and the white stone walls.

Abruptly the hallway opened out into a room that faced the lush, discreetly lit garden. A white grand piano stood near the windows, a woman in a silver gown seated at it, playing.

Grouped around the room were yet more of those long white couches, with people—women mostly, in beautiful dresses—sitting on them.

In the middle of the room was a big white armchair and sitting in the armchair was a man.

He had a woman curled in his lap while another draped herself over the arm of his chair, and he looked like a king on his throne. Or maybe a pasha sitting at his ease surrounded by his harem.

Glory stopped short in the doorway, transfixed.

He wore tailored black trousers and a white shirt open at the neck and he was quite simply the most beautiful man—no, person—she'd ever seen.

It was him. It was Castor Xenakis, and he was even more incredible in person than he was in his pictures.

His hair was a dark tawny colour, like a lion's pelt, and artfully tousled, his skin golden. His features looked like they'd been hand carved by Michelangelo himself, with an Attic profile, high cheekbones and a beautiful, sensual mouth.

His eyebrows were dark, his lashes thick and silky and streaked with gold, and his eyes were the same dark golden brown of fine brandy.

He was like an exquisite Renaissance sculpture that had been feathered with gilding and then given a light scatter of gold dust.

Glory quivered at the beauty of him.

He sat back in the chair, smiling at the blonde in his lap and curling a lock of her hair idly around one finger, while the brunette sitting on the arm of the chair leaned down to say something in his ear.

He laughed in response, the sound low and sexy, making a curious heat prickle all over Glory's skin.

Her breath caught, her stomach dropping right down into the red patent stiletto sandals that she'd picked up from a cheap chain store the day before, as something she'd already thought about but hadn't fully taken on board became clear.

He might be dissolute, dissipated and morally bankrupt, but he was also beautiful. Stunningly, heartbreakingly so, and she… She was not.

He was a Greek god while she was a small, brown church mouse, and there was no way—*no way*—in the world he'd ever consider her pathetic little offer. Not only did he possess a charisma that burned like a forest fire, he was also surrounded by the most beautiful women Glory had ever seen.

Why on earth had she ever thought he'd look twice at someone like her?

But what about Annabel? She needs treatment.

Oh, she did. But Glory was going to have to think of some other way of getting money because this obviously wasn't going to work. And as for her own secret obsession and her even more secret desire… well, she could forget about that too, because that wasn't going to happen.

She needed to leave now, before she made an utter fool of herself.

On the point of turning around and heading straight for the front door, Glory froze as a pair of heavy hands came down on her shoulders, gripping her lightly, and she was aware of someone standing behind her. A man wearing an overpowering after-shave that didn't do much to mask the odour of stale sweat, cigarette smoke and another, musky smell that made her shiver with distaste.

'Ah, there you are, Red Riding Hood,' the man said, his accent thick and Eastern European–sounding. 'I've been looking for you everywhere.'

Fear iced her veins, her heart beating suddenly very loudly in her ears.

You're an idiot coming to a party like this on your own, looking for the biggest womaniser in the world. What did you think was going to happen?

Okay, so yes, she'd been naive and being desperate hadn't helped either. And now some horrible man was going to drag her off God knew where and no one here would help her, she already knew that much.

Still, she wasn't going to stand there and let herself be taken. The stilettos might have been cheap, but she was betting that the man holding her wouldn't like it if she drove one of her heels into his foot.

Glory tensed, preparing to bolt. Then the breath stuck in her throat as Castor Xenakis's gaze locked on hers and she was held captive by a pair of golden-brown eyes, the distaste she'd felt at being grabbed by the man behind her scattering in a shower of bon-fire sparks.

An expression she couldn't name rippled over Xenakis's beautiful face before his gaze shifted to the man behind her. He smiled. 'Dimitri,' he said,

his voice deep and rich and warm as melted honey.
'I think Red Riding Hood might be a bit too tame
for your tastes. How about I find you someone more
interesting, hmm?'

Castor was furious, though he didn't let even a hint
of his fury escape. He prided himself on no one being
able to tell what he was thinking, still less what he
was feeling, especially in the middle of one of his
parties.

Most especially not when that party was turning
into a complete failure.

The people he'd invited—a group of known
human traffickers from Eastern Europe—had decided at the last minute not to come, sending only
Dimitri, a thug not only low on the totem pole but
also low in intelligence, in their stead.

It was an insult, that was clear, and it meant they
weren't taking any of his efforts to gain access to
their inner circle seriously enough.

He'd been trying for months to get close to this
particular group of traffickers, but it turned out that
the terrible reputation he'd careful cultivated, that
had enabled him to gain their trust as far as it went,
was now working against him.

This group were staunch family men, all with
wives and children, and they did not want someone
of Castor's ilk joining them. It drew too much attention, apparently.

It was beginning to be clear to Castor that if he

wanted to become one of them, he was going to have to do something to change their opinion of him.

He wasn't sure quite what that something was yet, but he'd do it.

Once he was part of that inner circle, all he needed then was to get the location of their next 'shipment' and pass that on to the authorities so they could intercept it.

He was going to take those animals down and their loathsome organisation with them.

Starting with that bastard Dimitri.

Are you sure you want to go after them now? In public?

That was true. How disappointing. He would have to settle with discretion, then.

His gaze fell once again on the woman Dimitri was holding. She was very small and wrapped entirely in what was, indeed, a red cloak. Her face was pale and sharp and fox-like, and she had the largest, most liquid dark eyes he'd ever seen. Eyes that had been full of fear as they'd met his.

The people that came to his parties were carefully chosen. They had few boundaries and even fewer inhibitions, and if any of them were frightened at being handled by Dimitri, none would have been gauche enough to show it.

But not this woman. Her fear was written all over her face.

She doesn't belong here.

Castor's temper, already roused, began to seethe. He always checked his guest list rigorously and people who weren't on it didn't get in, and he was pretty sure this woman, whoever she was, hadn't been on it.

So what she was doing here and how she'd got in, he had no idea.

What he did know was that he needed to get her out of Dimitri's clutches and fast. The man was a brutal thug and Marie—who was ex-military and one of his security staff—would know how to deal with him.

'Interesting?' Dimitri echoed, frowning. 'How interesting?'

Castor bent and murmured in Esme's ear, 'Off me, sweetheart. I'll come and find you later.'

Esme slid off his lap without a protest and he got up, sending Tyler, who was playing the piano, an apologetic look.

Then he turned and headed for the doorway where Dimitri stood with Red Riding Hood, those dark eyes of hers getting rounder and rounder the closer he got. As if she'd never seen anything like him before in her entire life.

A small pulse of…something went through him, though what it was, he couldn't tell. Strange. Lots of women looked at him that way. Women lovelier than she was, so why he should feel anything at all God only knew.

'Come,' he said easily, taking Dimitri by the arm. 'Let me tell you about Lola.'

Dimitri frowned, but let go of the dark-eyed woman. She was trembling slightly. Castor couldn't help but notice.

What on earth was she doing here? His parties were infamous, exclusive and wildly debauched, and they were not for the faint of heart.

What they were for was getting information from human traffickers about their operations so Castor could pass that on to the authorities.

It was not a place for someone who didn't know what they were doing.

Marie, luckily, was standing near the doorway, dressed in a tight black cocktail dress that showed off her magnificent figure at the same time as it gave her room to move if there were any threats.

Castor signalled her and she approached, smiling at Dimitri. 'Hi there,' she murmured, taking him by the arm. 'I'm Lola. Wanna go have some fun?'

Dimitri relaxed, letting her take him off down the hall, leaving Castor with Red Riding Hood in her cloak.

She was still very pale, staring up at him with those huge eyes. And he was conscious that his fury was in no way satisfied now Dimitri had been dealt with. In fact, for some reason he couldn't quite pinpoint, he was even angrier than he'd been a moment ago.

She wasn't one of his guests, which meant she'd somehow sneaked in. And that was dangerous not only for her, but for him as well. Especially if anything happened to her. He had an agreement with local law enforcement that they would leave his parties alone in return for the information he passed on, but if something happened to an innocent, even they wouldn't be able to ignore it. And that would put at risk everything he'd spent the last ten years working for.

'I—I—' she began.

'As for you.' Castor took her arm in an iron grip. 'You're coming with me.'

He didn't want to do this publicly. He would take her into his private study, where he could find out exactly who she was and what she was doing here, and then ensure she'd never make such a foolish mistake again.

She stiffened as he urged her down the hallway, but she was no match for his strength and was soon hurrying along beside him, her cloak fluttering out behind her.

His study wasn't far and it had a lock so no curious guests could blunder in.

He paused outside, pressed his finger to the fingerprint pad and heard the click as the door unlocked. Then he ushered her inside and shut the door behind them.

It was a pleasant room, not that he stayed in this house often since he spent most of his time in Europe. But he liked the windows that looked out over the garden rather than the sea. It had the same white walls; however, most of these were lined with sleek modern shelving housing the many books he liked to read. There were comfortable couches scattered around, plus a few roomy armchairs, and the lighting was all recessed and discreet.

The woman had pulled away to stand in the middle of the room, her cloak wrapped tightly around her, big eyes peering at him from the depths of her hood.

He couldn't tell what kind of figure she had, but she had an interesting face. Sharp chin, sharp nose, but the most gorgeously full mouth.

She looked scared so he put his hands in his pockets, keeping his posture loose and unthreatening, since although he was angry and determined to give her a piece of his mind, he wasn't going to hurt her.

That was the very last thing in the world he'd do.

'Sweetheart,' he said coolly. 'You shouldn't be here.'

She gazed at him warily, as if he was a rabid dog who might attack at any moment. 'I—I—I know. I wasn't invited.' Her voice was low, husky, and sent the most disturbing shiver of sexual awareness down his spine.

How inconvenient. Still, it wasn't an issue. He had Esme for tonight and she was always up for anything.

'No, of course you weren't invited. I know everyone on that guest list and you weren't on it. So tell me, who are you and what the hell are you doing in my house?'

She stared at him for a moment, then squared her shoulders as if bracing herself for a distasteful task and took a step towards him.

'Actually,' she said. 'I'm here to make you an offer.'

It wasn't unusual. Lots of people made him offers.

Castor raised an eyebrow. 'You gatecrashed my party to make me an offer? What kind of offer?'

'I'd like to offer you…' She lifted her chin as if she was facing down a firing squad, then dramatically threw off the cloak. 'My virginity.'

CHAPTER TWO

Surprise rippled over Castor Xenakis's phenomenally handsome face, and Glory might have found that satisfying if she hadn't been so utterly terrified.

First that awful man putting his hands on her and then the man she'd been obsessing about for months grabbing her arm and forcing her down a hallway into this room.

Now her heart was nearly coming out of her chest and she didn't know why she'd thrown off her cloak. Hadn't she decided she wasn't going through with this stupid plan?

It had only seemed as if now she was here, now she'd finally got him alone, she had to do it, because she didn't want to be a coward. Even if she had no hope of him ever accepting her offer.

A part of her even hoped he'd refuse. Mainly because Castor Xenakis as a picture in a magazine was a whole lot easier to deal with than Castor Xenakis in the flesh, standing right in front of her.

He was devastating. That was the only word for it. And he terrified her, though she wasn't sure why.

What she was sure of was that she wanted to get away from him as quickly as possible.

What about Annabel? What about the IVF? What about a night with him?

She would never get her night, that was clear to her now, and even if she did, she probably wouldn't be able to handle it anyway.

But Annabel…that was a different story.

'I beg your pardon?' he asked in his smooth, dark voice. 'You want to offer me your what?'

He'd been sexy in those pictures in the gossip magazines, been charming in all the interviews she'd read. He'd never denied his lavish parties or his exploits with his many lovers. And when he'd been accused of being shallow, he'd only smiled as if that was of no concern.

Yet while the man who stood in front of her was still sexy, he wasn't smiling now and the sexy charm he'd displayed out in the room with the piano was long gone. His gaze was razor sharp and there was no give in his fallen-angel face.

That should have made her more afraid, should have made her bolt from the room, because this man was harder and colder than the one in the magazines she'd read so avidly.

Yet she didn't move, standing there exposed in the skin-tight cheap red dress she'd bought in the hope it would showcase her figure, conscious of the strangest shiver of delicious anticipation running down her spine. As if part of her was relishing the chance to do battle with him.

'I—I w-want to offer you my virginity,' she repeated, annoyed with herself for stuttering. 'For a price.'

He stared at her and if she didn't know any better she would have said that he was slightly dumbfounded.

'Of course.' There were traces of a lilting, musical accent in his velvety voice. 'Your virginity, how novel.'

His obvious sarcasm generated a spark of anger inside her.

If he didn't want her, he should just say. He really didn't need to be quite so rude.

'Okay, fine,' she said, not stuttering now. 'It's clear you're not interested. Just forget I said anything and I'll be on my way.' Then she reached for her cloak.

Only to have warm fingers wrap around her wrist.

She took a sharp breath, realising belatedly that he'd moved, crossing to where she stood and so fast she'd barely had a chance to be aware of it let alone get away from him.

'No,' he said flatly. 'I don't think you will.'

Glory trembled, a strange combination of fear and excitement tangling inside her. 'L-let go of me.'

He didn't move and he didn't release her. 'Who are you? Tell me why you're really here.'

There was an odd intensity to him. He seemed... angry. Almost as if he thought she was lying to him.

'I did tell you.' She tried to pull her hand away. 'I came here to—'

'You really expect me to believe that nonsense?'

He looked so forbidding, his amber gaze cold. So very different to the man she'd seen talking to the woman in his lap just before, who'd smiled and then laughed that low, sexy laugh.

Yes, he was angry, she could see that. But did gatecrashing his stupid party really warrant scaring her like this? And what did he care anyway? He was rich and powerful, so why didn't he get his security to deal with her?

Glory hated confrontation so she didn't often allow herself to get angry. And when she couldn't avoid a confrontation, she usually dealt with it by staying quiet until the other person had finished ranting, before apologising profusely.

Yet for some reason, there was something about this man that made her usual apologies stick in her throat.

He was *very* angry, which didn't seem fair, plus there was the fact that he was completely, devastatingly good looking. She already knew about that—she'd been mooning over him and his looks for months after all—and yes, he had quite the sordid reputation, but did he have to be so unpleasant to her?

She was only an ordinary woman in the wrong place at the wrong time.

He could just let her go, not stand there interrogating her like she was a terrorist or something. Especially when all she'd done was gatecrash.

'It's not nonsense.' Glory felt compelled to point out, since it also wasn't fair he didn't believe her when she was telling the truth. 'That's what all the gossip magazines say. That you choose a woman to spend the night with and then you give her money or gifts or jewellery or whatever.'

He remained expressionless, his amber gaze never leaving her face. 'The gossip magazines. I see.' Unexpectedly, he let go of her hand. 'Your name, please.'

A small, rebellious part of her, the part that wanted to stand up to him, also didn't want to tell him, which made no sense, because it wasn't like her name was a state secret.

'Glory Albright,' Glory said with some dignity.

He nodded, then reached into his pocket and brought out a sleek-looking phone. Glancing down, he touched the screen, then turned, raising the phone to his ear as he took a few steps away from her.

Glory looked at the door, then back at the man standing not too far away from her, talking into his phone in a low voice. If she was quick, she could get to the door and get out of this room before he had a chance to move.

Except that won't help Annabel. Or get you what you want either.

It wouldn't, it was true. Then again, this whole virginity thing had clearly been a stupid idea from the start, and given his surprise when she'd offered it to him, either the rumours were wrong and he didn't choose lovers at his parties, or he didn't want her. Whichever it was, the outcome was still the same:

Annabel would not be getting her IVF treatment and she'd remain a virgin.

An odd pain shifted inside her and she swallowed, glancing back at him. He wasn't speaking English, but some other language she didn't recognise, low and musical.

Greek maybe? That's where he was from, wasn't it? Or at least, that's where the magazines had said. Maybe they were wrong though.

You should have known better than to believe them.

Of course she should have. She prided herself on being practical and keeping her head down, doing what she had to do.

That's what she'd done when Annabel had got sick, the small college fund that she'd put aside for Glory having to be used to pay for the cancer treatment. Not that it covered even a minuscule proportion of it.

Glory had had to drop out of school and get a job so the two of them had money to live on, since Annabel had been too sick from the chemo to work. Not that Glory minded. She hadn't wanted to go to college anyway, and besides, her sister was more important.

It was very good luck that the Jessups' little grocery store wasn't far from where she and Annabel lived, so she could walk to work, and they hadn't minded that Glory had no qualifications. She was polite, quiet and a hard worker, and that's what mattered most.

Gatecrashing a billionaire playboy's party and offering him your virginity is hardly polite and quiet.

No, that was true, it wasn't. Nor was arguing with him. She didn't like making people angry or upsetting them, and clearly she'd done both, which meant she needed to apologise for that and for ruining his party.

Glory drew herself up, steeled her spine and turned to him.

Only to find he'd finished on the phone and was standing there with his arms folded, watching her with that intent, almost predatory gaze.

It was unnerving.

She opened her mouth to apologise.

'Your name is Glory Albright,' he said before she could get a word out. 'You're twenty-three years old. You live at number 2A in the Bella Vista apartments. You dropped out of school to work at Jessups' grocery store, where you've been for the past few years. You have an older sister called Annabel who is currently in remission from breast cancer; you have a large amount of medical debt and no insurance. Correct?'

Glory stared at him, dumbfounded.

His gaze glittered in the light and she had the oddest feeling that he hadn't really looked at her before and that he was looking at her now. *Really* looking at her.

Her in her cheap red dress and cheap red stilettos, and the stupid cloak she'd found in a sale bin in the thrift store. Her with her untidy, unmanageable curly hair that never did what it was told and was probably already coming down from the bun she'd tried to put it in.

Her in the cheap make-up she'd had to borrow from Annabel, that she didn't know how to apply very well because she never wore it herself.

Glory Albright, the checkout girl who thought she had what it took to seduce a man as powerful as Castor Xenakis.

It was exposing having him know who she was. Know every little thing about her. It made her feel vulnerable and small, and vaguely ashamed of herself, though she had no idea why.

She wasn't ashamed of who she was or the life she and Annabel had managed to build after their parents' deaths. They had a roof over their heads and food on the table, and she had a job that while it didn't pay much, it was at least steady and the Jessups were nice people. And Annabel was in remission. That was far more than some people had.

Glory stared back. 'Yes,' she said. 'That's me. And for the record, if you'd wanted to know all of that, I would have told you. You only had to ask.'

His gaze flickered. 'I could, it's true. But forgive me, sweetheart. I don't know you from a bar of soap and you could have told me anything. A background check from a trusted source was necessary.'

He had a point. Still, she didn't really understand why that was necessary. Unless he thought she was a journalist or something. Perhaps he didn't want the media leaking details of his parties everywhere.

Then again, those details were already in the public arena so what was he being so cagey about?

Why do you want to know at all?

Oh, she didn't want to know. What she wanted was to get out of here, get home and then figure out what other options there were as far as getting money for Annabel's treatment. And as for her obsession, she'd simply have to deal with it. Perhaps she'd find another man who could help her move on. A man who was more in her league.

'Well,' Glory said. 'Now you know. So can I go, please?'

'Not yet, I think,' he murmured, gesturing at the couch behind her. 'Take a seat, Miss Albright.'

An icy current snaked down her spine and she had to fold her arms over her thumping heart. Because why would he want her to do that? Why wasn't he just letting her go? What did he want from her?

His gaze narrowed. 'I'm not going to hurt you,' he said. 'I just want to talk to you.'

His tone needled her, though why she wasn't sure. Maybe it was only that he'd picked up on her fear and she didn't like it. It made her feel even more exposed.

'I know.' She tried to keep her voice level. 'What I don't know is what on earth could you possibly want to talk to me about.'

Once again, his amber gaze moved over her, more slowly this time. Then the hard expression on his face eased, one corner of his beautiful mouth curving in a slight smile, as if he'd seen something about her that amused him.

'Well, mainly,' he said. 'I'd like to reiterate the dangers of wandering around parties you weren't invited to and offering your virginity to complete strangers.'

Glory felt her cheeks heat, that smile of his catching on her temper. She didn't know what was going on with her or why she was suddenly acting out of character and arguing with people she shouldn't be arguing with, but it had to stop.

Yes, he was overwhelmingly attractive, but he'd frightened her. And now he was looking at her in a way that made her skin feel tight and prickly, and everything in her was telling her that this was one confrontation she didn't want and she should get away from him and quickly.

Except the rebel in her wouldn't let her run.

He tilted his head, studying her, dark brows drawing together slightly as if he found her puzzling.

Glory was disturbed to find that she liked that very much, since very few people found her puzzling. Very few people thought much about her at all.

'How impolite of me,' he murmured. 'I know all about you, but you don't know me, do you?'

'I kn-know who you are,' she said, hating how she kept stammering and not understanding why she was still standing here. 'You're Castor Xenakis.'

He inclined his head. 'I am. Pleased to meet you, Miss Albright.'

'Pleased to meet you too, Mr Xenakis.'

'Call me Castor.' He nodded at the couch. 'Please, sit.'

'Oh, I think it's probably time to—'

He gave her a pleasant smile. 'I'm afraid I'm going to have to insist.'

Glory Albright was very pale, her dark eyes almost black. She was still scared, undoubtedly, which had been his aim, even though he hadn't much enjoyed doing so. He didn't like scaring women.

Then again, she had to know what a phenomenally stupid thing it had been to gatecrash one of his parties, and then to add to the stupidity by offering him her virginity. An idea she'd somehow picked up from some ridiculous gossip magazines.

It was ridiculous. It was also a concern.

He cultivated the rumours about himself very carefully, making sure the press knew only what he allowed them know, which was that he was a playboy of the worst kind, notorious for his appetite for women and wild parties. A man with few boundaries and no scruples who'd sell his soul for a good time.

It was a careful front he'd maintained for the past couple of years, which had allowed him to get close to various crime lords and gain access to information that would normally be impossible to get. Information that pertained to human trafficking.

Personally, he didn't care about his terrible reputation, that had ended up with him being tarred with the same brush as those unsavoury people.

It was the mission goal that counted and his mission goal was to help as many people affected by human trafficking as possible, in particular women.

And if being thought of as a dissolute playboy was the only way he could help those women, then that's what he'd do. Without a second's thought.

However, what he didn't want was for innocents like Glory Albright to start wandering into his parties thinking they could get money or kudos or whatever the rumours the gossip magazines were printing from him.

If anyone found out what he was really doing at his parties, then there was the potential for his cover to be blown, and the network of contacts and information he'd so painstakingly built would be destroyed.

Which couldn't happen and especially not when he was on the verge of gaining access to the biggest trafficking ring in Europe.

He needed to decide what to do with her that wouldn't involve her talking to anyone else, or coming back here with yet more ludicrous offers.

Do you have to do anything with her? She's not going to say anything. You could just let her go.

He could. But if anything the last ten years of associating with the scum of humanity had taught him it was that you couldn't trust anyone. People lied all the time, which meant you had to be careful. So very careful.

He had to find out if she'd run into anyone else tonight, or whether she'd heard anything she shouldn't, because he didn't necessarily want her running to the media with lurid tales of human traffickers and criminals.

Not that she'd be believed, he suspected. She was just a checkout girl at a grocery store with a sick sister. No one notable or special. A nobody.

A nobody in a cheap, stretchy red dress who happened to have, now that he was looking, a knockout figure. Generous breasts and hips, and a small waist. A classic pin-up.

Her hair had been covered by the cloak and when she'd flung it off, glossy, chestnut curls had fallen out of the bun it had been pinned in, some falling behind her ear and some haphazardly down to her shoulder.

It should have looked untidy but it didn't. It looked sexy, as if she'd been pulled into an alcove and ravished within an inch of her life.

From out of nowhere came the absurd impulse to go over to her and start pulling the pins out of her bun so he could watch all those luscious curls fall down over her shoulders. Then maybe bury his fingers in it just to see what it would feel like.

But he wouldn't, of course. Getting excited about an ordinary young woman who'd been reading too many gossip magazines? What a ridiculous thought for a man of his jaded tastes.

He'd seen everything, done everything. Nothing surprised him these days, nothing delighted him. Because after all, you couldn't live as long as he had in filth before some of it touched you, no matter how careful you were.

She was giving him a deeply suspicious look, as if she knew exactly what was going on in his head, in which case no wonder. He deserved her suspicion.

You scared her quite a lot.

Perhaps more than necessary. Clearly he'd let his frustration at the lack of progress with this particular trafficking ring and his anger at Dimitri get the better of him.

Another reason—as if he needed another—for him to figure out an alternative plan. Normally keeping a tight leash on his emotions wasn't a problem, but if he was letting fools like Dimitri get to him, then he needed to do something.

'I'd like to offer you some refreshments,' he said more gently this time. 'By way of an apology for scaring you.'

Her dark, liquid gaze was wary. 'You didn't scare me,' she said.

A lie. Her fear had been obvious. Which meant that perhaps it was time to give her the charming playboy rather than the wolf's sharp teeth. After all, it wasn't her fault she didn't know what these parties were really all about.

Deliberately, he relaxed his posture, let the tension bleed out of him. Put on the mask he'd cultivated over the years, the easy smile and the warm expression that didn't come naturally to him, but that he'd been faking for so long it was now part of him.

'I suppose that's why you keep looking at me like I'm going to murder you at any second, hmm?' He let amusement colour his voice.

She frowned, clearly not finding his sudden change in mood convincing. 'You might,' she said slowly. 'I've heard a lot of things about you.'

She had a point. Still, he hadn't thought his reputation was quite *that* bad if people thought him capable of murdering innocent gatecrashers.

Didn't you though? All those years ago? Wasn't it essentially murder?

Deep inside, an old agony stirred and along with it an old fury. But with the ease of long practice, he ignored both emotions, keeping his smile firmly in place.

'It's true, I'm not at all trustworthy,' he said easily. 'But since I'm Greek and we would rather die than let a guest under our roof suffer even the most minor of discomforts, you can trust in my sense of national pride at least.'

She eyed him warily for a long moment, a deep crease between her brows. 'Okay,' she said at last. 'I suppose I can do that.'

Sitting on the couch he'd gestured to, she grimaced as the hem of her dress rode up before instantly tugging it back down again. But not quick enough to prevent him from catching a glimpse of a pair of rounded, creamy thighs.

Sudden and unexpected heat caught at him and all at once he was again far more aware of her lush little body than he should have been. Of the indentation of her waist and the swell of her hips and thighs, outlined to perfection by that cheap red dress.

An ordinary young woman she might have been, but there was nothing ordinary about her figure.

Still, if he wasn't as notorious as his reputation made him out to be, he wasn't far from it, and if he wanted a woman he had her. However, he had rules. He always found his lovers from amongst his own social circle, experienced women who were out for some fun and nothing more.

Innocents were out of bounds and he'd never found that to be an issue.

It wouldn't be one now.

He forced his gaze from her hips, pulled his phone from his pocket and sent a quick text to one of his staff members ordering that some refreshments be brought. Then he sat down on the couch opposite her.

'So, Miss Albright,' he said conversationally. 'I hope you didn't run into anyone else causing you trouble tonight?'

Her straight, dark brows drew down again. 'No. Should I have?'

'Some of my guests aren't entirely polite. I wouldn't want you to have been inconvenienced by any of them.'

She shook her head, another long russet curl coming loose from her bun, and he found himself watching it as it fell slowly over her shoulder. The reddish gleam in the strands contrasted beautifully with her creamy skin.

'I wasn't inconvenienced, but thank you for asking.'

He wouldn't have thought a gatecrasher come to sell him her virginity would have such manners. Apparently he was wrong. Politeness wasn't a common commodity in the circles he moved in and he found it refreshing.

Relaxing on the couch, he stretched his arms out over the back in a conscious effort to put her at her ease, noting how she followed the movement of his body.

Interesting. He knew what that surreptitious look was all about. He knew that very well. And he wasn't surprised. He had a certain effect on women, and no doubt for this little sharp-faced checkout girl, he was dazzling.

Perhaps you can use that?

It was a thought he'd had before. Many times, in fact. He'd used his looks and the charm he'd forced himself to learn to pull himself up out of the Athens tenement he'd come from. After Ismena had disappeared and his mother had died.

He'd been called manipulative in his time and if manipulative meant his cause was more important than people's feelings, then yes, he was manipulative. Especially when his cause was to save as many people as possible from the fate his sister had suffered.

But she has nothing to do with Ismena.

This was true. And besides, what could he use her for anyway? She was a nobody.

'And you didn't hear anything that frightened you?' he asked absently, turning over various plans in his head, trying to figure out what his next move would be.

He couldn't make any progress with taking down this particular trafficking ring if he couldn't get information about their shipments. And he couldn't get access to that information if he wasn't part of the inner circle of people who ran it. So how to get access to that inner circle? They were, bizarrely, all family men with wives and children, and apparently didn't trust playboys like him.

In which case perhaps he needed to find himself a wife. Any marriage would have to be legal, naturally enough, in case anyone got suspicious and investigated it, but it didn't need to be for ever. Just long enough for him to get the information he needed to take this trafficking ring down.

Yes, maybe that was an option. Finding a woman who'd agree to marry him wouldn't be an issue either, since he had women coming out of his ears. Then again, if he married, focus would fall on his wife, which could potentially put her in some danger and he didn't like the sound of that. A beautiful wife in particular would draw the wrong kind of attention, so if he was going to take that route, he'd have to find someone who was plain enough that people wouldn't bother. Someone who wasn't famous either, someone whom no one else knew.

Someone…ordinary.

Someone like her.

Castor blinked.

Her. Glory Albright, checkout girl. Who'd been trying to sell him her virginity.

Interesting. Very interesting indeed.

She was looking at him from underneath lashes caked thickly in cheap mascara, wary still, but also curious if he wasn't much mistaken.

'You must need money very badly,' he said abruptly. 'If you were willing to sell yourself to me.'

'Oh…I…um…yes.' She folded her hands nervously in her lap.

'To pay back all your medical debt?'

'Um…partly.' She folded her hands again. 'Does that really matter?'

It didn't, but he was curious. Because whatever the reason, it was important enough to her that she'd do something so obviously out of character as to wander into his lair.

You could use that.

Yes, he could. And he had no compunction about doing so, not when the lives of people taken by human traffickers were on the line.

Ignoring the question, he asked instead, 'Why did you think I would choose you? Why did you think I would even pay you?'

'That's what the gossip magazines said and that you never sent a lover away empty-handed.'

'It didn't occur to you that they might lie?'

'Of course.' Her nervously shifting hands stilled and she looked at him. 'But I thought it was worth trying.' Something glowed in her eyes. Something he recognised: determination.

He liked that. He'd done a few things himself that were long shots, but he'd tried anyway, because he was determined. Because even though he'd found no trace of his sister in all the long years he'd been searching for her, he still wanted justice. To take down those responsible for her abduction.

Did this woman have a mission too? Perhaps he'd find out.

'Indeed,' he murmured. 'And what would you have done if I didn't pay you?'

Her expression became very serious. 'I would have appealed to your better side.'

Humour that he didn't have to force for once wound through him, and he smiled, because really, she was such an innocent. 'You're assuming I have a better side.'

'Everyone has a better side, Mr Xenakis,' she said in the same serious tone, her gaze holding his, dark and velvety and soft.

And he found himself wondering if she really believed that. If she could see past all the filth he'd buried himself in. See past the despair the years of false hope had given him. If she could see who he'd used to be before the mission had consumed his life, before he'd lost Ismena...

Then again, when hadn't his mission consumed his life? Everything he'd done, every decision he'd made since he was fifteen years old, had been entirely about finding his sister.

Who even was he without it? Perhaps she knew, perhaps she could see. Perhaps this plain woman, this nobody, could tell him...

No, you need to get back on track. Forget about what you need, this is about justice for Ismena.

That was true. In which case he had plans for Miss Glory Albright.

She was a plain woman with an ordinary life, not

a celebrity, not famous and very definitely not rich. And she could be exactly who he needed.

Yet, when he spoke, it wasn't the proposition he'd intended that came out of his mouth, but something else instead. 'Do you really believe that?' he heard himself ask, his voice gone a little rough. 'Do you really think everyone has a better side?'

She didn't hesitate. 'Of course. Some people's are more hidden than others, but everyone has one.' Her sharp little face suddenly softened, her mouth getting full and lush, and she smiled. 'For example, yours is quite hidden, I think. But it's there. It's definitely there.'

He didn't believe her, but he liked that she so obviously did.

She's not for you, fool.

Oh, he knew that, not that he wanted her, of course. At least, not in that way. But he could definitely use her and he would.

Castor leaned forward, his elbows on his knees, hands clasped between them. 'That's good,' he said. 'Because I have a proposition for you.'

CHAPTER THREE

GLORY WAS UNNERVED. Castor Xenakis's intensity was back again, a fierce glitter in his eyes that made her breath catch.

She couldn't look away.

A moment before he'd seemed to relax, the hard look on his face easing, his mouth curving in a smile. He was once again the charming man she'd seen flirting with the woman in his lap out in that room.

Except she suspected his charm was a mask he wore, that he could put on and take off at will. How she knew that, she wasn't sure, especially when he was still a stranger to her. But that was the thing about being polite and quiet. You got good at observing people, and since they pretty much forgot you were there, it was interesting watching how they reacted and how they behaved when they thought no one was looking. You got good at seeing things in them they probably didn't mean to reveal, secrets they thought they could hide.

She could tell this man had secrets, just as she could tell that despite his infamous reputation, he wasn't a bad person. A bad person wouldn't have cared Dimitri had touched her. A bad person would have let Dimitri take her away, not interrupted his evening to save her.

It didn't mean he wasn't dangerous though, because whatever secret he was hiding, it seemed… painful. And she couldn't help being drawn to people in pain. She wanted to help them, wanted to make them feel better, and that wasn't something she should be doing for him.

He was notorious, a powerful stranger, not to mention disturbing in a way she couldn't put her finger on, and if she was sensible, what she should be doing was getting out of here, not listening to his proposition.

Perhaps you could use it to help Annabel?

Well, that was true. Perhaps she could.

'What proposition?' Glory asked cautiously.

His posture was casual, his long-fingered hands loosely clasped between his knees. Yet he seemed to vibrate with an intense, leashed energy, as if he was barely holding himself back from exploding into movement.

She had no idea why she found that so attractive, but she did. Then again, everything about him seemed designed to appeal, and not only to her but women in general.

'How would you feel,' he said, 'about marrying me?'

Glory blinked. Marry him? What? Surely she'd misheard. 'Excuse me?' she asked. 'I'm not sure…'

'You heard right.' His dark golden stare and the sheer perfection of his face were far more mesmerising than they had any right to be. 'I'm asking you if you'd considering marrying me.'

She blinked again. He couldn't be serious. He couldn't.

'I...I don't understand,' she began hesitantly. 'Wh-why would you want to do that?'

He remained perfectly still, energy crackling around him. Looking at her as if the very fate of the universe depended on her answer.

She'd never been looked at that way before. Never had anyone stare at her with so much intensity, seeing her. Really *seeing* her.

It was disturbing and thrilling and frightening, and she didn't know what to do with herself.

'I have a...project that's important to me.' His voice was coloured with that warm richness she'd heard out in the living area. 'And the success of it involves presenting a certain facade. However, that facade does not mesh with my current reputation, which means I need some way of improving it.'

Glory frowned, not understanding. 'What kind of project? And how is marriage going to improve your reputation?'

He made a dismissive gesture. 'The project itself is confidential for a number of reasons. And as for my reputation, I'm hoping marriage to someone like you will improve my standing with certain...people.'

She frowned, her brain somehow skipping over the vague parts of his statement and settling on the thing that probably didn't matter. 'What do you mean, someone like me?'

He smiled the fake smile that he probably thought was charming, that he probably thought no one saw through. 'I meant no offense. It's only that you're not famous or rich, or powerful. You're a perfectly ordinary young woman, which in my world makes you rather...extraordinary.'

Glory already knew she was nothing special, she'd always known that. But for some reason she didn't like this beautiful man pointing it out to her.

You want to be special. Special and not a burden.

She ignored that thought, unfamiliar anger gathering inside her. 'Um, thank you,' she said and then, before she could think better of it, added, 'Though that's not really a compliment, is it?'

His smile flickered like a flame, warm and bright. And maybe if she hadn't been as sensitive to people as she was, she would have been charmed by it. But she could see the darkness behind that smile. It didn't quite reach his eyes.

And it came to her suddenly that it wasn't that horrible Dimitri who was the wolf in this scenario.

It was this man sitting in front of her.

'I'm not looking to compliment you,' he said. 'I'm looking to pay you.'

'Pay me?'

'What? You think I'd ask you to marry me out of the goodness of your heart? No, sweetheart. I won't pay you for your virginity, but I'll certainly pay you any sum you care to name for your hand in marriage.'

Glory could feel her heart thumping painfully hard behind her breastbone, shock moving slowly throughout her entire body.

When she'd come to this party, she'd thought it would only involve one night. She'd thought that if she somehow managed to catch his eye and he agreed to her offer, she'd lose her virginity in the best way possible: to the man she'd been admiring and desiring for months now.

But this was…not that. This was marriage in aid of some project he'd said was confidential. It seemed bizarre and strange, and considering his reputation, she shouldn't touch this offer with a ten-foot pole. Especially when it was clear a night with him wasn't on the table, which she couldn't help feeling disappointed about.

Except…he was looking at her so intently. As if he was desperate for her to say yes. As if he even needed her, which was odd considering he could have any woman he chose. He didn't specifically have to have her.

Does it matter why he wants you to marry him? If it means Annabel can have her treatment, then it doesn't matter.

True. As long as it wasn't anything illegal, of course, or something that would end up hurting someone.

He didn't say anything more, watching her, leaving the ball clearly in her court.

When he'd asked her whether she really believed he had a good side, she'd got the impression it was something he wanted to believe himself but didn't. She did though, even if she wasn't quite sure why.

Annabel called her naive sometimes and too optimistic for her own good, and maybe that was true. But trying to make the best of things and always looking for the silver lining had helped make things easier for her sister, who wasn't a bright-side kind of person.

'Well,' she said at last, still doubtful, yet at the same time oddly reluctant to disappoint him by refusing, 'This project of yours isn't illegal, is it? And it's not going to hurt anyone?'

Slowly, he shook his head.

'Okay,' she murmured. 'So…how would it even work?'

The corner of his mouth curled in the most fascinating way and it felt genuine this time, as if her answer had amused him, though she wasn't sure why. 'It'll be a marriage of convenience only and for… say, a year or two, not for ever, if that's what you're worried about. This would purely be for show.'

'Does it need to be legal though? You need an actual marriage?'

'I do. The people involved in this project might investigate and so I will need documentation to prove I am actually married.'

A shiver of unease went through her. 'What people? Investigate how?'

'I can't tell you that. Or at least, not yet.' The fierce glitter in his eyes burned. 'Well?'

He was driven, she could see that immediately.

It was clear by the look in his amber gaze and in the vibrating, leashed energy that crackled around him. Driven by what, she had no idea, but whatever it was, it certainly drove him hard.

Curiosity tightened way down deep inside her. What on earth would compel a man like this one? A man who had everything. Everything she didn't. Ah, but it must be to do with that secret she'd sensed in him, that aura of pain.

You shouldn't be quite *so fascinated by him.*

No, she shouldn't. Especially when all those questions she kept asking herself weren't going to help her obsession with him.

Yet…she couldn't help herself. There were so many terrible rumours swirling around him and yet he didn't seem to be quite so bad in person. And that intrigued her probably far more than it should.

You should refuse him.

Maybe. Then again, there was Annabel.

Her sister had always wanted a family of her own and while cancer and her treatment had interrupted her plans for finding a partner, it had also sharpened her desire. She wanted a child before when and if the cancer returned, and Glory wanted to help her get her wish. She wanted it desperately.

'So…' Glory said carefully. 'What exactly would it entail?'

A smile lingered around his mouth. 'I'd need you to ostensibly live with me—we can stay in LA if you'd prefer, so you can be close to your sister. And then after a year, we'd get a divorce. I would arrange everything, all you would have to do is pretend to be madly in love with me.'

She stared at him in shock. 'What? Why?'

He seemed to find her response even more amusing, because his smile deepened and this time it did reach his eyes, making her feel hot, as if her skin was too tight for her body. 'I did mention the word "pretend" did I not? I only need the appearance of love, *mikri alepou*. I need this to be believable. The story of an ordinary girl capturing my heart, making me change my wicked ways and become a good family man will do wonders for this project of mine.'

She swallowed. 'I don't know... What did you call me?'

His expression softened. 'Little fox. It's Greek.'

'F-fox?'

He ignored her. 'Think of the money, Miss Albright. This wouldn't involve your virginity. You wouldn't have to sleep with me. I won't demand anything from you but your signature on the register and your presence for a couple of weeks. Nothing too onerous.' He tilted his head, gazing at her from beneath gold-tipped lashes. 'I have an island in Greece that would make a lovely wedding venue, so wouldn't you like a vacation? Some time in the sun? Perhaps you'd even like to go to Europe for a honeymoon, see some monuments.'

Her head was spinning and she wasn't sure if it was his offer or just him and the way he looked at her. Not the charming smile or the practised warmth, but the ferocity she could sense just below the surface of him. The wolf hiding in the skin of a man.

Hungry, that was what he was, though what he was hungry for, she had no idea. It wasn't sexual, she didn't think, but then how would she be able to tell? No one had looked at her like that before. No one ever had.

What does it matter that he wants a marriage? It's not for ever. And you'll get a couple of nice weeks' vacation and Annabel will get her dream.

That was true, but he'd also mentioned how he wanted whoever these people were to think theirs was some kind of great love story. Which would involve her pretending she was in love with him, and how was she going to do that? She might be obsessed with him, sure, but that wasn't love. Plus, she'd never been good at pretending.

Aren't you though? Haven't you been pretending your whole life? Pretending you didn't mind that Annabel had to give up her dreams for you. That dropping out of school to care for her was exactly what you wanted. That working at the Jessups' was a good, steady job. That you didn't have dreams of your own...

Glory shut those thoughts down hard. Her dreams were of a steady job, earning enough to live on, paying off her debt and making sure Annabel was happy. That was it.

'I don't care about vacations,' she said flatly, because it felt important that he know that. 'I'm not doing this for me.'

His mouth quirked in a cynical smile. 'Of course you're not.'

'It isn't like that,' she insisted. 'All of this is for my sister. For IVF treatment. She wants a baby.'

'A baby,' he repeated, frowning, as if he didn't know what the word meant.

'Yes, she had breast cancer. It's in remission now and so she wants to try for a child. She brought me up after our parents died and so I'd…I'd like to do something nice for her.'

Why are you telling him all this?

She had no idea. The words just kept coming. 'I mean, she had to give up a lot of things for me and then she got cancer, which really wasn't fair so I thought I could make sure that at least one of us got what we wanted.'

Castor leaned back against the couch again, his long legs stretched out under the coffee table. Again, he seemed relaxed, but she knew he wasn't, not with those fierce wolf eyes looking at her.

'Only one of you?' he asked lazily. 'And what is it that you wanted?'

You want him. That's what you want.

'It doesn't matter what I want,' she said tartly, ignoring that thought too, because she certainly wasn't going to tell him that. 'Annabel wanted a child as soon as she could in case her cancer came back.'

He was quiet for a long moment, studying her. Then he said, 'I'll pay for your sister's IVF. As many rounds as it takes, and also for any follow-up treatment. I'll clear your medical debt and any other debt too. You have my word.'

Her mouth went dry. All those debts, that terrible mountain of money that there was no hope of her ever paying back in her lifetime, crushing her, crushing Annabel, just…gone.

She could hardly imagine it.

'It's a l-lot of m-money,' she croaked.

He smiled, practised and charming, as if it was no big deal. 'Then isn't it lucky I'm very rich?'

'You can't possibly—'

'Of course I can.' That brow lifted again. 'Well? Do we have a deal, Miss Albright?'

Glory's eyes had gone round with shock, her hands clenched on her thighs.

He couldn't blame her. Money solved a lot of problems and it was clear from the look on her face that those problems had been large ones. He knew that feeling though, where you realised that all the things that had been hanging over you, the insurmountable difficulties, were suddenly gone.

He'd felt that way after he'd made his first million. The heady rush of knowing there was only one direction to go in from here and that was up. More money, more power. He wasn't that fifteen-year-old boy trying to find his sister in the chaos of the Athens streets. Going from place to place hoping someone would help. But nobody had because nobody cared, not even the police.

He was poor and alone and probably lying, so why should they?

It had been in those dark days after Ismena's disappearance that he'd decided. He'd taken his eye off her for one second and she'd gone, so he wouldn't make that mistake again. He would be focused, intent, and he'd pull himself out of these streets. He'd get all the money and power, and then he would find her.

So that's what he'd done. And that's what he was doing even all these years later, still trying to find her. Still trying to save other people—women mainly—who'd been caught in the net. He wouldn't let any other brother, father, uncle go through what he had, and he'd use whatever he could to achieve that.

Including the young woman sitting opposite him.

Hope was a difficult commodity to hang on to, or so he'd found, but if marrying this woman was what he needed to do in order to take down that trafficking ring, then he'd do it without a second's thought.

This woman with her soft, dark eyes and her assurance that everyone had a good side…

She was certainly determined, and he'd liked very much how loyal she was to her sister. It made him think of himself and how far he'd gone for his, and how far he was still prepared to go if he could even find one hint that she was still alive.

Glory's pretty mouth had firmed, the wrestling match she was obviously having with herself clear in her expression.

Well, he hadn't expected her to agree immediately despite the incentive he'd offered. It was already plain she wasn't of his world where money ruled and people would do anything for a taste of power including selling themselves.

She'd come here to do the same thing, with no idea of the cost it would exact. No idea of the scars it would leave, because the things you did when you were desperate always left scars.

Are you sure you're that desperate? Marrying you will put her in danger.

It would, but he had the resources to protect her. And in a year or so, once the fuss of the marriage had died down, no one would even know who he was married to, he'd make sure of it. She could fade back into the obscurity she'd come from.

And yes, he was that desperate.

'You want an answer now?' There was a deep crease between her brows. 'I really need to think about it.'

Unfamiliar impatience twisted in his gut.

'What do you need to think about?' he asked. 'Fundamentally, *mikri alepou*, what it comes down to is this: it's either worth it for you or it isn't.'

Her hands clenched on her thighs again, drawing attention to the soft round shape of them beneath her dress. More hair had come down from her ridiculous bun, curls lying glossy and gleaming a deep reddish brown over her skin. She had little freckles scattered over one shoulder, disappearing under the strap of her dress and he was gripped by a sudden, intense urge to shift that strap to one side so he could see them better.

He shifted, impatience tangling with the heat collecting inside him, making him feel restless and agitated.

Really, what was it about this woman that got him so hot under the collar? He never normally had such problems ignoring what was basically a mere physical attraction.

She didn't seem to notice his tension, letting out a breath and catching her full lower lip between her teeth. And despite himself, he found his gaze drifting to the press of her white teeth against the soft, red fullness of her mouth.

If he were to bite her like that, would she taste as sweet as she seemed? Like honey? Or would she taste more like sugar?

Why don't you bite her and find out?

The thought drifted like smoke through his head and for half a second he found himself contemplating it. Of charming her, seducing her. Burying his hands in her curls, taking that soft lip between his teeth, and biting down. Not too hard. Just enough to make her gasp and maybe—

Theos, what the hell was he doing? That was *not* happening.

Glory huffed out a breath, her chin firming as if she'd made a decision.

Castor forcibly corralled his wayward thoughts and lifted a brow questioningly.

'Okay,' she said. 'Fine. I'll do it. I'll marry you.'

A spike of satisfaction caught him, sharp and bright, though he made sure not to let it show. 'Excellent. In that case, I'll get the necessary—'

'But I have some requirements.' She gave him a severe look, as if she expected him to argue.

He almost wanted to, just to tease her, but now was not the time for games. 'What requirements?' he asked instead, without inflection.

Glory held up a finger. 'First, I'd like the money for my sister's first round of IVF right away, because the sooner we start, the more chances she'll have. Secondly.' She held up another finger. 'I need your assurance that this is a marriage in name only. I d-don't want to…sleep with you.'

First a stutter, then a hesitation. What was that all about? She was a virgin so it could just be discomfort with the subject of sex. Then again, hadn't she come here intending to offer him sex? Yes, she'd been nervous in her offer, but it wasn't as if the thought of sleeping with him hadn't crossed her mind.

What did she think about that?

Why do you want to know? You're not going to sleep with her after all.

Well, no, he wasn't. Yet even though it wasn't the time for games, Castor couldn't help himself. The temptation to test her was too irresistible. 'Are you sure? You didn't seem to mind the prospect when you came here to sell your virginity to me.'

She reddened, but to her credit didn't look away. 'I *didn't* want to sleep with you. I was prepared to do it for Annabel's sake, that's all.'

He might have believed her if she hadn't been blushing and if that protest hadn't sounded just a touch hollow.

'Quite the sacrificial lamb, aren't you?'

'Not at all,' she said with quiet dignity. 'I don't mind. My sister is important to me and I want her to have some of the things she missed out on.'

That sobered him. Because if there was one thing he understood, it was the importance of one's sister.

'Very well.' He dropped the teasing tone. 'The money issue won't be a problem, and I'm certainly not going to be demanding my marital rights from you. However, as I said, I want this to look as real as possible, and while that won't entail actual sex, it will require more than a handshake.'

The marriage had to look real even if it wasn't. It had to stand up to scrutiny in case anyone got suspicious of him and decided to investigate. Certainly once word got out, the press would be interested and if there had to be pictures, he wanted pictures of a couple in love. Nothing else would be convincing.

Her dark eyes narrowed. 'What more are we talking about?'

'Have you never watched a pair of lovers, *alepou mou*? Do you really not understand what's involved?'

Irritation flashed over her face, which intrigued him. She might have been afraid before, and definitely nervous now, but it seemed as if she was comfortable enough with him to be annoyed at him.

'I understand, Mr Xenakis.' A small, dark flame

of temper burned in her eyes. 'I might be a virgin and rather naive, but I'm not stupid.'

He could feel another unexpected smile curving his mouth, which was unheard of. How strange. Genuine amusement was something he thought he'd lost years ago.

'You should probably start calling me Castor,' he reminded her gently. 'I'm not sure many women outside a Regency novel call their husbands "mister."'

More colour flushed her cheeks, turning them a very pretty pink. 'No, I suppose not,' she muttered. 'C-Castor.'

He didn't know why he liked the way she stuttered slightly over his name, but he did.

'Much better,' he murmured. 'However, to answer your questions, I suspect you are not, in fact, stupid. And as to what more I require, obviously I'm going to need to touch you.'

The blush made her eyes seem even darker. 'Touch me? Touch me how?'

He was being deliberately opaque and he knew it. Mainly because he'd forgotten how delightful it was to fluster a woman. It certainly didn't happen with the women he associated with these days. Women who were as jaded as he was and who didn't get either shocked or surprised by much. Oh, he flirted with them, but it was all rote, both his responses and theirs.

This wasn't though. Her responses were natural and delightful, and that blush… She sparkled when she blushed. He liked it. He wanted more of it.

'Well,' he said, dropping his voice into a low, seductive purr. 'I'll probably want to hold your hand. And maybe put an arm around you, pulling you close. Then quite possibly I might put a finger under your chin and tilt your head back. Perhaps I may even kiss you. For the cameras, you understand. Just a light brush across your lips, nothing too risqué.'

The blush in her cheeks became deeper and deeper as he spoke, but she didn't move, continuing to stare at him as if she'd never seen him before in her entire life.

'And after that, I might want you to do the same things to me. Hold my hand. Lean in close. Look at me as though you adore me. Kiss me as if you can't wait for a taste.' He met her gaze, held it. 'It's not sex. At the most it'll be a couple of kisses, I give you my word. So what do you think, *mikri alepou*? Is that something you'll be able to contemplate?'

Glory blinked. Raised a hand to her mouth and coughed. 'I'm not sure,' she said, her voice husky. 'I've never kissed anyone before.'

Surprise flickered through him. While it was clear she was inexperienced, he hadn't thought she'd be *that* inexperienced.

'No one?' he asked, more sharply than he'd intended. 'No one at all?'

She shifted on the couch in an irritated fashion. 'You don't have to sound *so* shocked. It's not that strange to not have kissed anyone before. I just never met anyone I was interested in. Anyway, I didn't have the time for boyfriends.'

'I'm not shocked. More surprised.'

'Why? It wasn't totally my fault. No one ever showed any interest in me. I mean, after all, you said yourself that I'm a very ordinary young woman.'

He heard it then, the soft edge of hurt in her voice. *You shouldn't have said that.*

No and especially not when he was starting to suspect that it wasn't true. Because if she'd been a very ordinary young woman, he wouldn't find the idea of flustering her quite so delightful, or the idea of kissing her quite so erotic.

'Does it matter what I said?' he murmured, watching her.

'No.' She looked down at her hands, a silky curl slipping over one shoulder and over the swell of her breast.

She was lying through her teeth.

There were too many things in Castor's life that he regretted. Too many things that were broken beyond repair. But this small hurt he could fix.

'I was wrong,' he murmured. 'I don't think you're ordinary after all.'

'It's okay, you don't need to lie.'

'I'm not lying. In fact, if you come over here I'll show you just how ordinary I think you are.'

CHAPTER FOUR

CASTOR'S SMOKY AMBER gaze burned from beneath dark, gold-streaked lashes, making it difficult for Glory to look at him without her breath catching.

He was just too…male, too beautiful. Too much of everything.

Why did you ever think you could handle him?

She had no idea. What she did know was that agreeing to this preposterous idea was a terrible mistake.

Yet, what else could she do? She'd come here for Annabel and the thought of leaving empty-handed was impossible. She had no other ideas about how to get the money Annabel needed. This was it.

And you want him too, don't deny it.

Okay, so she did. But that thought scared her. *He* scared her. Not that he would hurt her, not when he'd had plenty of opportunity to take what he wanted from her and hadn't. No, it was more about how fast her heart was beating and how tight her skin felt.

How she'd argued with him instead of apologising

and hadn't immediately done what he'd said without protest.

How hot her cheeks were when he'd talked to her about kissing her and about how she might kiss him in return.

She couldn't even imagine it.

Can't you? Can't you imagine getting up and moving over to him. Bending and kissing that beautiful mouth...

Her face flamed.

He tilted his head slightly, obviously taking note. 'What are you thinking about? Something nice? Perhaps something to do with me?'

'No. No, I—'

'Well?' One corner of his mouth lifted. 'Are you going to give me a chance to show you? Or are we going to do this at another time?'

'This?' Her brain wouldn't work. Nothing seemed to work, not with him staring at her like that.

'We need to be comfortable with each other.' His voice deepened into something that resembled a purr. 'Which means you're going to have to get used to me being close. I understand that this might be too soon, so if you don't want to do this now, we can leave it a couple of days.'

Him being close. The very idea of it...

I could hold your hand...tilt your head back...just a light brush across your lips...

She could almost feel it too, the press of his mouth to hers. It sent sparks cascading all over her skin.

No, this was insane. She was letting him get to

her far too easily. She needed to pull herself together, not sit there staring at him with her mouth open like a landed fish.

And being totally practical about it, he wasn't wrong. She did have to get used to him being close, especially if he wanted it to look real. So perhaps she should stop thinking about it and just do it. Get it over with. Besides, a kiss was the very least thing she'd thought she'd end up having to deal with tonight.

'No,' she said, then cleared her throat and said it again. 'No. Tonight will be fine.'

He shifted, a subtle movement that drew her attention to the length of his muscular body. To the white cotton of his shirt pulling tight over the width of his wide shoulders and broad chest, and the wool of his trousers constricting around his powerful thighs.

Oh, holy…

'Are you sure?' His voice wrapped around her like warm velvet. 'Like I said, we can wait a day or two if you'd rather.'

He's putting it on, all this charm. You know that, right? He's trying to seduce you.

The thought caught at her like a thorn and she glanced at him, looking past the blinding charisma, directly into the dark amber of his gaze.

And she expected to see the same cold deliberation she'd seen when he'd smiled at her initially, how the warmth didn't touch his eyes.

She was even bracing herself for it.

But it came as a shock to find it wasn't there. Neither was the warmth. Instead there was something far hotter, an ember of that fierceness she'd seen lurking beneath the surface of his charm. An intensity that made her throat close.

Why though? And what did it mean? Was he attracted to her?

It seemed impossible that a man of his beauty and power could feel anything at all for an ordinary woman like her, yet she couldn't get rid of the thought. It made her feel good. Made her feel… strong. As if, perhaps, she might be able to handle him after all.

'No,' she said slowly, staring back at him. 'I think tonight is good.'

Then she pushed herself to her feet.

He watched her a moment, then slowly did the same, rising to his full height in a graceful, athletic movement.

Scraping together the remains of her courage, Glory took a couple of steps in his direction, then stopped, her heart thumping.

Amusement filled his gaze and it was genuine. 'You'll have to come closer than that, *mikri alepou.*'

Little fox…

She'd never had a nickname. Never had anyone use an endearment. Annabel called her 'Glor' sometimes, and that was okay, but it didn't make her shiver the way she shivered when Castor murmured in Greek.

'Yes, I do know that, thank you,' she said, then

immediately felt bad for sounding cross. 'Sorry. That was rude.'

'You're very polite, aren't you?'

'Of course. It costs nothing and it makes people happy.'

'You like making people happy?'

'It's better than making them sad. There's enough sadness in this world already.' She wiped her palms surreptitiously against her thighs. 'So, what should I do first?'

'I think I suggested holding your hand.' He held his out, a hint of challenge in his eyes. 'Please tell me you've at least held hands with someone before.'

'No,' she said, because why bother lying?

The heat in his eyes wavered a second and he frowned, as if her answer had personally offended him somehow. 'What? Why the hell not?'

'Because I never met anyone I liked enough, I told you.' And it was true, she hadn't. Not when every single man she'd ever met had seemed to pale into insignificance compared to the Castor Xenakis she'd read about in her magazines.

'I see,' he said, sounding sceptical. 'Well, it's nothing to be afraid of.' He held his hand out more insistently. 'Come, *mikri alepou*.'

This was silly. If she couldn't even get up the courage to hold his hand, then how was she ever supposed to pretend to be his new bride?

Why did you ever think you could do this at all? It was a stupid idea and you know it, and Annabel would be appalled. You're just going to create more problems for her, like you always do...

No. *No*, that wasn't true. She was going to help her sister and if holding hands with this man, if marrying him, was what she had to do, then she'd do it.

Glory took a silent breath, lifted her chin and reached for his hand.

And all the breath left her lungs as his long, strong fingers closed around hers.

His skin was warm, his grip firm, and it was strange, but the second he closed her hand in his, something inside her relaxed at the same moment as something else gave a little thrum of excitement.

She blinked at the sensation and stared at him, searching his beautiful face, wanting to know if he felt it too.

His expression was opaque and even though he seemed relaxed, there was a tension to him. She took a step closer, curious to know what was going on, but his lashes swept down, veiling his gaze. 'And now,' he murmured. 'I'm going to put my arm around you and pull you in close.'

Before she had a chance to move, he lifted his other hand, sliding his arm around her waist and drawing her into his side.

She tensed, waiting to feel uneasy at being so close to him. Yet the unease didn't come. Instead there was only a restless heat and a fluttering excitement that crowded in her throat.

Because beneath his lashes, his gaze had turned

smokier, brighter gold glinting in the amber depths, a glimpse of the wolf.

The excitement fluttered harder, that rebellious part of her liking that she could rouse the predator in him. A scary thought, yet also thrilling.

Did he feel this too, then? This heat? This excitement? Or was it all only her?

Castor drew her in closer until she was barely inches away. He towered over her, all wide shoulders, broad chest and hard, masculine strength, and she should have felt threatened by it, but she didn't. She felt safe and almost…protected, which was a strange thing to feel when this man's reputation had him being a predator of the worst kind.

He smelled warm, of that exotic spice, and for absolutely no reason that she could see her mouth watered.

She blinked up at him, fascinated by that wolfish glint in his eyes.

'How is this?' His voice was soft and deep, a caress of rough velvet.

'G-good,' she stuttered breathlessly.

He kept his gaze on hers as he slowly lifted her hand and brought it to rest on his chest, holding it there in his own warm grip.

She took another shaky breath, aware of the warm cotton of his shirt and, beneath that, the rock-hard plane of his chest.

'And this?' He looked down at her, gauging her reaction.

She'd never been this close to a man before, let

alone this man. Never had his arm around her waist, one palm resting gently in the small of her back, while his other hand held hers to his chest. Never been pressed lightly against the length of a hard, masculine body, never felt his heat.

She'd fantasised a little about what it would feel like to have him touch her—nothing beyond a few light kisses since she'd found the thought of anything else too overwhelming—but the reality was... different. So much hotter. So much more exciting.

If you feel like this now, what will a kiss do to you?

Oh, nothing but destroy her in the best possible way.

'It's good,' she whispered, because it was, and this time she didn't stutter at all.

Castor released her hand, but kept holding her. 'Now, what did I say I'd do? Oh, yes... I lift your chin and tilt your head back.'

There was a warm fingertip beneath her chin, exerting a light pressure, easing her head back so she was looking directly up into that fascinating dark golden gaze of his.

It was obvious now, that fierce glitter. That... hunger, and for some reason it was fixating on her. She didn't know why. What there was about her, plain old Glory Albright, a checkout girl in a tiny grocery store, that made him, one of the most notorious playboys in the world, look at her like that.

Whatever it was though, it terrified her. It also left her trembling with excitement and a hunger that came from somewhere deep inside. A hunger that was entirely selfish, and not at all quiet or polite. A hunger for what came next, because she knew what that was. He'd told her. A kiss.

She quivered, waiting.

Except he didn't move, his gaze glinting gold.

Glory took a breath, then another. But still he waited. And a surge of impatience went through her. Because she didn't know why he was holding back and she didn't want him to.

He was so very close. All she'd have to do to reach that beautiful mouth would be to go up on her tiptoes. It wasn't far, not very far at all…

She'd come here for Annabel, it was true. Yet right in this moment it wasn't Annabel she was thinking about, but herself and what she wanted.

She was thinking about all those months of obsession and desire for something she could never have. About how she could have that now if only she had the courage. And she did have it. That's why she was still here after all.

So Glory rose up on her toes and pressed her mouth to his.

He went very still.

His lips were warm and softer than she'd expected, and they felt as amazing against hers as she thought they would. He smelled delicious and she was fascinated by the heat seeping through the cotton of his shirt and into her hand. Was he as hot like that everywhere? Was he as hard?

Her breathing was coming very fast and she wasn't sure what to do next. How, exactly, did you kiss a man? She'd obviously seen kissing before on TV, but she was pretty sure that it wasn't actually like that. You were supposed to do something with your tongue, weren't you?

You idiot. You're going to make a total ass of yourself.

A sudden wave of embarrassment at her own inexperience washed through her. Annabel had always told her she was too impulsive, that she needed to be more restrained, and this was in no way restrained.

He probably hated the kiss. He probably thought she was ridiculous and silly.

Blushing, Glory came down off her tiptoes. 'Sorry,' she muttered and tried to pull away.

Except he didn't let her go. If anything his grip on her firmed, holding her right where she was.

'Glory, look at me.' His voice had gone very deep and even rougher than before, and this time there was an unmistakable command in it.

She didn't want to look at him, didn't want to see what she knew was going to be distaste in his expression, but she was helpless to resist the command.

His eyes had gone a deep, brilliant shade of gold. 'Kiss me again, *mikri alepou.*'

Castor stayed very still, every instinct screaming at him to let her go. That this was a mistake. This was *all* a mistake. And he'd known it the moment he'd taken her hand.

Her skin had felt so soft and warm, her hand small, fitting his palm to perfection. And she'd looked at him with such wide eyes, as if holding his hand had been the most amazing experience of her life.

Drawing her closer had felt natural and even with his instincts telling him not to, he hadn't been able to stop. He had to anyway, he'd told himself. They couldn't pretend to be in love without touching each other and she needed to be comfortable with him.

Now he was touching her, holding her, and she'd just about brought him to his knees with an expected kiss.

He couldn't believe it. It had hardly even been a kiss. And he wasn't sure why he'd responded to it so powerfully, yet the moment her soft mouth had pressed to his he'd felt as if she'd lit him with a match and he was about to go up in flames.

Chemistry, of course, though why he should have it with this sweet little innocent who had no idea how to even kiss properly was a complete mystery.

As was why he was still holding her when he was close to breaking point.

As was also why he'd commanded her to kiss him again, as if another kiss was the answer to this dilemma.

Wonder glowed in her eyes as she looked up at him, her cheeks fiery with her blush, her freckles like stars scattered over her skin.

He'd thought her plain initially, yet now he was struggling to understand why when it was so obvious that she wasn't plain in the slightest. Unusual, yes, but not plain. Not with that creamy skin and those dark, velvety eyes. That determined chin and that full little mouth.

She gave him a worried look. 'Are you sure?'

He could see her pulse at the base of her throat. It was beating fast yet she wasn't scared. She'd been scared before, when he'd brought her in here, but she wasn't now.

She was warm in his arms, her soft curves pressing deliciously against his hard angles, her scent very feminine, sweet and citrusy. Was that her perfume? Body lotion? He liked it very much.

'Kiss me,' he said roughly, the impatience he'd been struggling to deal with getting the better of him. 'Now.'

'But I'm not very good at—'

He took her mouth again before she could finish and all thought left his head.

She didn't resist and automatically he firmed his grip on her chin and took control, at first staying still to let her get used to the feeling, before he moved his mouth on hers slowly, showing her how it was done.

She'd stilled, and not, he thought, out of shock, but as if she was simply waiting for more. So he gave her more.

His tongue touched her lips in a brief taste. And then a couple more times. Touching the corner of her mouth and then the centre, before following the line of her lower lip. Then a few butterfly kisses, light brushes of his mouth on hers, tantalising her.

She trembled, her breath catching.

His hunger growled, but he ignored it. For some

inexplicable reason he was close to the edge and he refused to let himself go over, not for one kiss given to him by a virgin.

No, he'd go carefully, show her a little more and then pull back. This was her first kiss after all, if what she'd told him was correct, and there was no point in scaring her.

But then Glory blew all his plans out of the water.

She slid both her arms around his neck and opened her mouth beneath his.

Heat engulfed him, the fire she'd lit leaping high, and slow and careful and gentle went abruptly out the window.

He pushed his tongue into her mouth, kissing her hard, chasing the sweet taste of her and finding yet more heat, yet more sweetness. He began to explore, hunger building inside him, and before he knew what was happening, his hands were where they'd wanted to be since she'd first thrown off that ridiculous cloak, buried deep in her hair. It was as soft as he'd imagined, like raw silk.

He closed his fingers in it, tugging her head back further, tasting her deeper as heat expanded between them. She melted, pressing all those soft, lush curves against him, making a desperate little sound, as if she wanted to get even closer to him, but still wasn't close enough.

In the back of his mind, something screamed at him that he was making an even bigger mistake, but somehow it got lost under the sudden explosion of desire that was pulsing through him. The desire to push her up against the wall, drag up the hem of her dress and bury himself inside her. Lose himself and forget for a few brief minutes the mission that consumed his every waking thought and the loss that wouldn't leave him alone.

Her arms tightened and he was achingly aware that the soft heat between her thighs was pressing against the front of his trousers. Against his aching sex. It made him growl deep in his throat, made him let go of her hair and put a hand to the small of her back, fitting her more firmly against him.

She sighed into his mouth, kissing him back, still inexperienced, yet bolder now, with a sweet edge of demand that made him want to give her everything she was asking for.

Then she gave a little gasp, wriggling against him, and he realised with sudden shock that he *had* pushed her up against the wall. But she wasn't wriggling to get away, she was wriggling to get closer, pressing herself against him in a way he knew well.

She wanted him. She was desperate for him.

You can't do this. You can't take her. Where the hell is your control?

He didn't know. Somehow it was gone. One young, inexperienced and ordinary young woman had made it disappear with a kiss.

Appalled at himself, Castor grabbed what was left of it—and it was disturbing how much strength even that took—and let her go, shoving himself away from her.

He was breathing hard—too hard—and before he

knew what he was doing, he'd put a hand through his hair and had begun adjusting his clothing like a prim Regency miss who'd just been taken advantage of.

Glory was leaning against the wall, her eyes dark, her cheeks flushed, her mouth full and red from the effects of that kiss.

She looked shell-shocked and he was gripped by a sudden, sickening doubt that she hadn't wanted this, that he'd taken advantage of her, that the company he kept had stained him irretrievably and he couldn't be trusted.

Yet before he could get a word out, she said, 'I'm so sorry, Castor. I shouldn't have done that.'

For a second he could only stare at her, not understanding what she was apologising for when all of this had been his fault.

'Why are you sorry?' He knew he should temper his voice, make it gentle, make it warm and charming. But there was no charm left in him. 'I shouldn't have pushed you up against the wall, and I shouldn't have asked for that kiss. And I should be the one apologising.'

Glory looked stricken. 'Why? What happened? Did I do it wrong? It was probably terrible. I've never kissed anyone before so no wonder—'

'Wait.' He held up a hand, trying to understand what on earth she was talking about. 'What do you mean "it was probably terrible"?'

She was making small fluttering gestures with her hands as if she didn't know what to do with them.

'I…well… It's just that it was no wonder you pushed me away. I'm not very good at this.'

'You think I ended the kiss because it was terrible?'

Her cheeks had gone even redder, making those pretty freckles stand out. 'Isn't that why? You didn't want my…uh…what I was trying to sell you earlier and then I just kind of k-kissed you and—'

'Stop,' he ordered and even though he knew it was probably better for both of them if he let her believe he hadn't been moved by that kiss, he couldn't lie to her like that. 'Let me be clear. I didn't end that kiss because I wanted to. I ended that kiss because I wanted to keep going.'

Her mouth opened, her gaze wide and shocked, as if she didn't quite believe what he was saying.

'And now,' he went on. 'Since I have a fair few things to organise, I'll let Corinna see you home. I'll be in touch, Glory Albright.'

Then before she could speak, he turned and strode from the room.

Before he changed his mind and continued where they'd left off.

CHAPTER FIVE

GLORY SPENT THE next couple of days half thinking what had happened in Castor Xenakis's mansion was a dream. That she hadn't really gone there offering to sell him her virginity. That he hadn't got angry and refused her, before suddenly turning around and asking her to marry him for…reasons he then wouldn't tell her. And that she hadn't taken his hand, risen up on her toes and kissed him.

A kiss that had set her entire world on fire.

It was too bright a memory. Like the sun, she couldn't look at it directly without being blinded by the heat of that moment.

His mouth on hers. The demand of it. His hands in her hair, exerting the most delicious pressure. The feel of his body, hard and strong and so hot. The way he'd kissed her, as if he wanted to consume her whole…

It was everything she'd ever imagined and her entire being shivered in response.

Then he'd looked at her like he'd never seen anything like her in his entire life. As if she was something totally new and different and he didn't know what to make of her.

She'd liked that. She'd never been new and different to anyone before, still less a man as experienced and worldly as him. And yes, she'd liked that *very* much indeed.

She'd been delivered home that night in a sleek black car driven by one of Castor's staff members, and as she'd stumbled into the run-down apartment she shared with Annabel, she'd felt oddly like Cinderella. Except the car had disappeared into the LA night instead of turning back into a pumpkin, and her dress and shoes remained, looking as cheap and tacky as they had when she'd put them on at the beginning of the evening.

She'd told Annabel before she'd left that she was going out with friends, which her sister had been vaguely suspicious of since Glory didn't really have friends, but luckily Annabel had been asleep by the time she'd let herself inside, so she didn't get the third degree about her evening.

Half bracing herself for it the next morning, it was a relief to find Annabel too distracted about some email she'd just received to be concerned about Glory's night out. The email had apparently informed her that she was the lucky recipient of a special grant from a charity who helped cancer patients achieve their baby dreams with subsidised IVF.

Glory blinked in surprise as Annabel relayed all of this, because she'd never heard of such a charity.

But as Annabel went on excitedly, Glory realised that there was only one person who could have organised it.

Castor. And he was making good on his promise.

Relief flooded through her and she had to look away so Annabel wouldn't see it. Because not only had he kept his word, he'd done it so that Glory wouldn't have to make any uncomfortable confessions.

Of course, the tricky thing now was that since he'd upheld his end of the bargain, she was going to have to uphold hers.

The thought made her feel scared and excited at the same time. Scared because it was marriage she'd promised him, and excited because he'd mentioned travel, which she'd always wanted to do, and…well… *him*.

'What's up?' Annabel asked. 'You're looking very pleased with yourself all of a sudden.'

Glory flushed. Great, now she'd have to think up some lie since she couldn't exactly tell her sister what was really happening. About how her IVF grant was really from an infamous playboy who was only paying for it because Glory had agreed to a marriage of convenience with him. *After* he'd refused to buy her virginity.

Yes, that would go down like a lead balloon.

'Oh,' she said, thinking frantically about what to say that Annabel would believe. 'I…um…entered a competition. To win a…European holiday. And I was just imagining winning it.'

Her sister, predictably, frowned. 'Oh, Glory. Really?' And there it was, the usual disappointment in her tone. 'I hope you didn't have to pay any money. You won't win, you do know that, don't you?'

How do you know that? Glory wanted to ask her sister. *The chances are small, yes, but just because they're small doesn't mean it won't happen.*

But this was an old argument. Her sister's glass-half-empty outlook and her determination to make sure Glory didn't 'get her hopes up' had been a constant in Glory's life. Normally she didn't bother quarrelling about it, since she didn't like upsetting Annabel, but for some reason today it needled her.

Because wasn't it better to have some hopes rather than none? Otherwise what was there to strive for?

Says the woman who has striven for nothing but working at the Jessups' grocery store.

Glory ignored that thought. There was nothing wrong with working at the Jessups' store. It was a good, steady job and it paid the bills. Perhaps one day she'd think about what else she wanted from her life, but that day was not today.

'No, I didn't pay any money,' she said, 'but you're probably right, I won't win.'

The next day, she was kneeling on the cracked lino of the tiny, narrow aisle of the store, stacking tinned vegetables, when she heard the bell above the door ring, signalling a customer.

Getting to her feet, Glory went down the aisle to the counter, only to come face to face with a man in an extremely expensive, elegant suit who gave her a judgmental up-and-down look before asking, 'Are you Miss Glory Albright?'

Trying to resist the urge to wipe her sweaty palms on her stained jeans, Glory nodded.

The man held out a white, thick-looking envelope. 'Your contract, Miss Albright. Mr. Xenakis wishes an immediate reply.'

She blinked at the envelope, reality suddenly crashing down hard. 'Oh,' she said stupidly. 'Immediately?'

The man inclined his head. 'Indeed. The contract has been looked over by an independent and neutral party, and Mr. Xenakis sends his assurances that it is all aboveboard.'

Glory took the envelope and stared at it.

You can't sign this. This is marriage you're talking about. Marriage to a man you don't even know, who could be every bad thing they say about him and more. It's a mistake and you know it.

It probably was. And as to marriage, well, he'd been clear it was a marriage of convenience only. It was almost like a…job. Yes, that's how she needed to look at it. Which meant that this was her employment contract. And anyway, she'd promised him she'd do this, and she always kept her promises.

Glory took the contract, signed it quickly and gave it back to the man, before she could second-guess herself.

There. It was done. No backing out now.

Not long after that, an email arrived in her inbox that contained nothing but a date and a time, a request for some details for a passport and an attached itinerary, detailing flights to Athens.

Athens. She was going to Athens.

Glory knew she should reply requesting more information, such as how long she'd be going and what to bring, and what about her passport since she didn't have one. But part of her didn't want to ask. Part of her was thrilled at the mystery of it, since mystery had been sorely lacking in her life up until this point.

She'd dreamed as a kid of princesses and castles, of dragons and white knights. She'd wanted adventures and expeditions, and fairy tales. But then her and Annabel's parents had died and all the adventures and fairy tales had died with them.

There had only been Annabel, tired and grief-stricken, trying to look after a flighty, dreamy and far too imaginative ten-year-old. Always telling Glory that she had to be quiet, behave, not talk to strangers, not sing in the hallways or fight pretend battles in the stairwells. That she had to stay in the background, keep her head down, stop being 'silly.' That dreams were nice, but reality was where everyone lived and that's where she had to live too.

Except not today. Because here was her adventure, staring her in the face. A fairy tale complete with a handsome prince. And while fairy tales weren't supposed to happen to ordinary people—as her sister liked to say—perhaps sometimes they did.

So Glory decided she wasn't going to ask for more information. She wasn't going to ruin it with boring, crappy reality. She was going to have her mysterious, thrilling adventure while she had the chance.

There were a few details she was going to have to figure out though, such as what to tell her sister. Annabel would definitely have words to say about a marriage of convenience to an infamous billionaire, but whatever those words were, Glory didn't want to hear them.

Annabel would worry and no doubt try to talk her out of it, and Glory didn't want to have to deal with either of those things. Plus, she didn't want to have to explain how she'd met Castor, not yet.

Which meant she was going to have to lie.

It wasn't ideal, because eventually her sister would find out the truth. But Glory needed some time to think about how to break the news that not only was she married, but she was going to be living in Castor's mansion. Then there was the question of her job and what she was going to do about that, but again, that was something she'd deal with later.

She took a couple of days to brace herself, then she asked the Jessups for some time off—which they grudgingly gave her—and then one night over dinner mentioned to Annabel that, actually, she'd won her competition and that she'd be flying to Greece next week.

Her sister was flabbergasted and Glory couldn't help feeling slightly smug, even though the whole competition thing was a lie.

'Well,' Annabel said after she'd spent some time grilling Glory on where, when and how. 'I'm pleased for you. I really am. You deserve something nice, especially after the past few years.'

Warmth spilled through her. Her sister was genuine, Glory could see that.

'Thanks,' she said, impulsively reaching for Annabel's hand across the table and smiling. 'You get your dream and I get mine. Didn't I tell you it would all work out?'

But Annabel didn't smile back. She squeezed Glory's hand, then pulled away. 'Don't go building castles, Glor. Reality isn't quite that easy.'

It stung that Annabel persisted in talking to her like she was a child, but Glory didn't say anything. There wasn't any point. And besides, her sister was probably right. It wasn't as if this ridiculous idea of marrying Castor Xenakis would result in any kind of happy ending, not when he'd mentioned a divorce at the end of it.

As he'd said, it would be a nice vacation in an exotic location, nothing more.

Still, that didn't mean she couldn't enjoy it.

She was more than ready a week later when the same sleek, black car that had taken her home that night at the beach house drew up outside the apartment again, this time ready to take her to the airport.

Annabel had some errands to run and so Glory had already said goodbye by the time came for the driver to load her single, battered suitcase into the trunk. So she had no one to wave goodbye to as they drove away, not that Glory was sorry for that.

The lie she'd told Annabel ate away at her. Because Castor was famous and if this was supposed to look real, she'd probably end up in the same gossip magazines he did, and even though Annabel didn't pay much attention to celebrity gossip, there was a chance she'd find out about it before Glory had a chance to tell her the truth.

The thought made her anxious, adding to the anxiety that already gathered in the pit of her stomach, along with a very real fluttering feeling that was probably excitement and of course had nothing whatsoever to do with *him*.

She'd been very good at not thinking of him at all the past week, not even glancing at the magazines in the rack next to the counter. Very good at not thinking about the kiss the night at his mansion either or about what would happen if he kissed her again.

'I didn't end that kiss because I wanted to. I ended that kiss because I wanted to keep going.'

Glory stared down at her hands in her lap, her heart giving a little kick as she remembered what he'd told her. He'd pushed her away so forcefully after she'd clutched at him, and she'd automatically assumed it was because she'd overstepped. But no, it hadn't been. He'd liked that kiss every bit as much as she had.

What if he hadn't ended the kiss? What if he'd kept going?

Her heart kicked again, harder this time, a sudden rush of heat scalding her cheeks.

No, she couldn't think about that. It hadn't happened and wasn't going to. She'd been very clear she wasn't going to sleep with him and not because she didn't want to. She *did* want to. But she was afraid he might decide he was mistaken when he'd told her that he didn't find her ordinary after all.

While he might have liked that kiss, a kiss wasn't sex, and she was *very* inexperienced. He'd be used to women who knew what they were doing, not check-out girls who didn't.

Not that this was about her in any case. This was about doing what she'd promised for Annabel's sake.

Glory found herself staring at a small stain on her jeans and it suddenly occurred to her that she hadn't bothered to wear something nice. She hadn't even bothered with make-up. She'd flung on some jeans and a T-shirt, grabbed an old sweatshirt, put her hair in a ponytail and that was it.

Yes, ordinary, that's what you are.

Well, and what was wrong with being ordinary? Nothing. She wasn't ashamed of it, and anyway, that's what he'd wanted, wasn't it?

A perfectly ordinary woman.

Glory ignored her cycling thoughts since they weren't helping, staring out the window and watching the city go past instead. And then gradually realised that they weren't going to LAX as she'd expected, but somewhere else.

That somewhere else turned out to be a small, private airfield where the car drove straight onto the runway and pulled up to where a sleek-looking Learjet waited.

Beside the jet stood Castor chatting easily to a woman in a pilot's uniform.

He was casual today, dressed in a pair of faded blue jeans and a black T-shirt. The hot LA sun glinted off the gold strands in his dark tawny hair and made his skin look even more gilded than it already was. Sunglasses hid the smoky amber of his gaze, but she could still remember the fierce heat in it as he'd stared at her after that kiss.

Her mouth dried, her palms sweaty.

If he'd been beautiful in simple black trousers and a white shirt a week earlier, in casual jeans, a T-shirt and sunglasses he was devastating.

A nameless fear suddenly filled her and if she'd been driving she'd have hauled on the wheel, turned right back around and headed straight back home again.

But she wasn't in her own car and she had no time to tell the driver she'd changed her mind and could he please take her home, because at that moment Castor turned his head, and even though the windows were opaque, it felt to Glory as if he was looking straight at her.

Her face flamed, memories of that night hitting her full force. The intense heat of his body. The warm, woody scent of his aftershave. The taste of his mouth, like brandy and dark chocolate and mint all rolled into one.

And her own response, the wild uprush of excitement and longing. A hunger for something she didn't have a name for, and the intense feeling of rightness, as if his arms were the place for her. As if he was the home she'd been fantasising about for so long.

No fantasies. No dreams. Stop it. You signed a contract. This is a job so do it.

Glory curled her fingers into fists in her lap as Castor broke off his conversation with the pilot, striding towards the limo with the intent, purposeful grace of the predator he hid behind that charming smile.

It made Glory's heart thump painfully with a complicated mix of fear and excitement, and the knowledge that she was going to have to interact with him and she had no idea how, not after that kiss.

Perhaps it would be better if she simply pretended it hadn't happened.

She plastered what she hoped was a natural smile on her face as Castor pulled open the door and then there he was, standing in front of her, as devastatingly handsome as he'd been that night at his mansion.

His beautiful mouth curved, his gaze remaining hidden behind his sunglasses. 'Good morning, Glory Albright.' His voice was exactly as she remembered it, deep and dark, like rough velvet rubbed against her bare skin. 'I hope you're ready for our flight. A press release has already gone out from my PR team and there are likely to be photographers around, so follow my lead as we walk to the jet.'

A press release. Photographers. Which meant she'd have to start acting like his lover right now.

All thoughts of the kiss and how she was going to handle interacting with him went by the wayside.

'The press?' She sounded squeaky. 'Here? Already?'

'Yes, already.' His smile shifted, a slight adjustment that made it seem less practised, more natural. 'Don't look so scared, *mikri alepou*.' There was a reassuring note in his voice. 'It's not far to the jet and I'll be with you.'

Glory pulled nervously at the denim of her jeans as the full reality of her situation descended on her in a way it hadn't before. There would be people watching her, people taking photos, and here she was, in a pair of old jeans and a T-shirt, her hair in a ragged ponytail…

'I'm s-sorry,' she stammered. 'I should have worn something nicer, put on some make-up or something. I just didn't think, and I don't have anything very nice to wear—'

'It's fine,' he interrupted, as if it wasn't a big deal. 'That's exactly how I want you to look for our first appearance together. Come on, let's get this over with.' And then he held out his hand to her.

It's not the photographers who are making you nervous.

No. It was the thought of taking his hand and how she'd feel once those warm, strong fingers closed around hers. Whether she'd lose her mind so completely the way she had before or…

'Glory.' His voice was very deep and very soft, jolting her.

She blinked, pulled herself together and took his hand. And once again as his fingers closed around hers, heat twisted inside her before erupting in little prickles all over her skin.

It almost made her jerk her hand out of his grip, but she managed to stop herself at the last minute. If he noticed, he gave no sign, pulling her out of the car and into the bright sun. Then she was being drawn slowly yet inexorably into the heat of his body, the scent of his aftershave surrounding her, making her mouth water.

Alarm must have shown on her face, because he bent his head as one powerful arm circled her waist, his hand resting lightly in the small of her back. 'I'm going to kiss you,' he murmured close to her ear. 'Just briefly, for cameras.'

Another kiss. Dear God, she better not embarrass herself again.

'Okay,' she croaked and closed her eyes, just to be safe. Being close to him was almost more than she could handle, let alone looking at him at the same time.

A fleeting warmth brushed over her lips and she found herself trembling. Wanting to go on her toes again and kiss him back, taste him the way she had a week earlier. Remind herself again of his rich, heady flavour. It would stay with her for ever, she knew, and even just thinking about it made her desperate for more.

Was there something wrong with her that she couldn't stop thinking about kissing him? That she couldn't stop thinking about wanting more? About exploring him to discover whether he was as hard as he looked, whether he was as hot. Whether his skin would taste—

'You look hot.' His voice had gone even deeper, a seductive roughness edging his tone. 'Perhaps we should get you somewhere cooler.'

Glory stiffened, feeling as if she'd let slip something she shouldn't. She wanted to pull away, but his arm remained securely around her and it wouldn't look good for anyone watching if she did, so she stayed where she was.

'I'm fine,' she said, her own voice sounding wooden in her ears.

He stared at her a second, his expression hidden by the sunglasses, then without another word, he turned for the jet, urging her along with him.

'That should give them a couple of good pictures,' he said. 'Thank you. You did well.'

There was a warmth in the words that made her stomach flip over, which was silly when he'd only said thank you.

'No problem,' she forced out.

This was crazy. Her mouth was tingling, every inch of her was exquisitely aware of him and there was an ache right down low inside her, between her thighs. A nagging, dragging kind of feeling.

She wanted to step away, put some distance between them. But she didn't dare, not when there were photographers around.

Castor ushered her up the stairs and into the jet,

and for a second she was distracted from his disturbing physical presence by the realisation that she was actually standing in someone's private jet.

His private jet.

Because this was Castor Xenakis, head of a billion-dollar corporation, as renowned in the boardroom as he was in the bedroom, and of course he'd travel by private luxury jet.

The interior was all pale carpet and cream leather, with low coffee tables in a dark wood. A pleasant, smiling woman in a pale blue uniform greeted them, but Castor murmured something to her and she soon disappeared off down the back of the plane, leaving him to guide Glory to her seat himself.

'I can do it,' Glory muttered, achingly aware of him as he leaned over to help her with her seatbelt.

'I know you can.' He pulled the seatbelt across her. 'Humour me.'

She wasn't sure why she had to humour him, but she didn't want to argue, so she let him fasten the belt in place before he mercifully stepped back and sat down in the seat facing hers.

Ten minutes later they were in the air and the smiles he'd had for her earlier were gone. It was as if he was a different person, the person he'd been that night at his mansion, angry and fierce and driven.

She'd been fascinated by him then, but now, given her own uncertainty, she wouldn't have minded seeing one of his smiles, even the practised ones.

'So, *mikri alepou*,' he said. 'I suppose now I should tell you the truth about why I want to marry you.'

* * *

Glory's soft, red mouth opened, then shut, her russet brows drawing together in puzzlement. 'But you've already told me. Something to do with a project, I think you said.'

Castor wasn't sure why he was talking to her about this or what had prompted him to bring it up. It was only that dressed in a plain white T-shirt and jeans with a couple of stains on them, and her curls in a haphazard ponytail, he'd been struck anew by how painfully not of his world she was. How unpractised and innocent, and how irresponsible it was of him to use her the way he was doing.

Yes, but you're doing this for Ismena's sake. You can't forget that.

It was true, he was. Yet leaving Glory in the dark didn't sit well with him, especially given how young and vulnerable she was.

Or how attracted you are to her.

He let out a silent breath.

This whole week he'd busied himself with his wedding plans, trying to forget about that kiss and how haunted he was by the heat of her mouth and how sweet she'd tasted. How she'd pressed her lush little body against his and kissed him back, hungry for him. And how he'd found himself pushing her up against the wall without even being aware of it.

He'd told himself that his loss of control with her had been an aberration borne of frustration at his lack of progress and that when he saw her again, that strange, uncontrollable hunger would have disappeared.

Yet it hadn't.

The same surge of desire had risen up inside him again the moment he'd pulled open the door of the car and her gaze had met his. Wide and dark and soft, and full of emotion. The effect had been like a lightning strike.

For a good many years he'd built up his reputation as the corrupt, jaded playboy, slowly lowering himself deeper and deeper into the mud so he could get close to the real criminals, all the while thinking he could keep himself clean.

But that had been a comforting lie. He didn't feel clean, he never had, not since the mission had consumed him. He knew other people saw him that way too. In fact, he couldn't remember the last time a woman had looked pleased to see him, excited that he was here.

He'd been forced to attend too many occasions where the bastards who trafficked in people displayed their 'wares.' It sickened him every time. And he'd had to bear the way those poor women had looked at him, as if he was like the men he was trying to take down. As if he was the enemy, the abuser, the brutaliser.

Yet he didn't see that in Glory's eyes. He saw desire and excitement, and yes, fear, but also a rising heat. The same heat he'd seen the night she'd kissed him.

It made him want to take her face between his

hands and demand she tell him exactly what it was she saw in him, ask her what that good side of him was, because he was starting to forget he had one.

But of course he couldn't do that, so he'd tried to ignore the feeling. At least until she'd taken his hand and their physical chemistry had kicked into life. And he knew his loss of control that night hadn't been an aberration. That what he'd felt then, he felt now, and it was her.

It was all her.

He hadn't been able to resist drawing her in close or pressing his mouth to hers in a brief, insubstantial kiss. He'd said it was for the press, but it wasn't. It had been for him.

That's all you should have. You don't deserve more.

Oh, he was well aware. And he wasn't going to touch her again, that was for sure. But he hadn't treated her very well that night, and she deserved an explanation.

No one knew his real mission—no one apart from the authorities and a few of his staff—because if it ever got out, he'd immediately lose the trust of the people he was trying to take down.

But he didn't think she'd tell anyone. He didn't trust many people—if he trusted anyone at all—yet he had the feeling he could trust her. At least with this.

'Yes, that's correct,' he said. 'It is part of a project.'

'What project?'

Such a simple question with such a complicated answer.

You'll have to tell her about Ismena.

The thought made something growl deep inside him, the part of his heart he kept locked away. The part that felt too deeply, that had never recovered from the wound her disappearance had left and still prowled obsessively around it, guarding it, protecting it.

He didn't talk about Ismena, not to anyone, because while she had long since vanished, he was still her big brother and he was still protecting her even if it was only her memory.

Glory's dark gaze was expectant, waiting for him to continue. Then abruptly concern rippled over it and she leaned forward, putting one delicate hand over his where it was resting on the arm of his seat.

'What's wrong?' she asked.

Shock jolted through him, both from her question and from the gentle touch, a lightning strike of emotion that felt like it lit him up inside.

Automatically he pulled his hand away from hers, the smile he used too often to distract people from asking too many questions already curving his mouth.

'Nothing's wrong.' His voice even sounded normal. 'Why would you think there was?'

Or maybe it didn't sound normal, because instantly she drew her hand back, the concerned expression on her face flickering.

'I…I'm sorry. I didn't mean to intrude.'

There's no need to snap at her.

He hadn't thought he'd snapped, but clearly he had. And she'd picked up on his thoughts of Ismena somehow, which meant he needed to manage himself better.

Still, he didn't have to mention her. He could tell Glory about the project without having to reveal his motives.

'It's fine,' he said dismissively.

Mercifully at that moment the stewardess interrupted to take drink orders and organise other refreshments, giving Castor a moment to pull himself together.

He undid his seatbelt and shifted in his seat to get more comfortable, stretching his legs out, crossing them at the ankle.

Glory had undone her belt too and kept giving him wary glances from underneath her lashes. He didn't miss how her gaze kept dropping to his body either, which made all his muscles tighten, made him think that perhaps he should keep the conversation light, flirt with her, tease her, seduce her.

Make it all about her so he didn't have to deal with the prowling grief that ached in his heart.

But flirting was too dangerous when he was in this mood, especially with a woman he had this level of chemistry with. And most especially when she was someone he shouldn't ever touch.

Besides, there was a part of him that wanted to tell her. That wanted to tell *someone* and why shouldn't it be her? She'd seen something good in him without him even having to do anything, so why shouldn't she know?

He was tired of keeping it to himself.

'The project I'm talking about is something I've been doing for the past ten years,' he said without inflection. 'And that is using my wealth to infiltrate some well-known and notorious European human trafficking rings.'

Glory's eyes went wide. 'Human trafficking rings?'

'It's undercover work of a kind, I suppose. I pass on any information I'm able to get onto the authorities who can then rescue the people being trafficked. However, there is one ring in particular that I need access to so I can get the information I need and my reputation is working against me.'

She was staring at him in shock, not saying a word, so he went on. 'The inner circle of this particular ring are family men, as ironic as that sounds, and they are wary of admitting anyone who doesn't have the same values. Hence me marrying you. I'm hoping that a declaration of love and a wedding will help them change their minds.'

There was a dumbfounded expression on her face. 'You're…kidding, right?'

Of course she wouldn't believe him. Why would she? When the facade he presented to the rest of the world was so complete?

'No,' he said, holding her gaze and letting her see the truth in his eyes.

She was silent a long moment. Then she said at

last, 'That's…amazing. Just…an incredible thing to do.'

He didn't know what he'd been expecting, but for her to not only take what he'd said at total face value but also think it was amazing was not it.

He shifted in his seat, uncomfortable for some reason. 'You believe me?'

She blinked. 'Why wouldn't I believe you?'

'People lie for all kinds of reasons, believe me, I know.'

'But you're not lying. I can see that you're not.' Abruptly she sat forward and her hand came out again, slender fingers resting on his knee. 'I told you that you had a good side.' Her dark eyes glowed. 'You're like…like the Scarlet Pimpernel.'

Castor had no idea what to say to that, especially when the light touch of her fingers was burning through the denim of his jeans, scattering his thoughts.

'Does anyone else know about this?' Glory went on, oblivious. 'The police obviously, but other people?'

'No. And the fewer people who know, the better.' He tried to ignore her hand. 'The only reason it works now is because the people who run the trafficking rings don't suspect me. I have such a terrible reputation for a reason.'

'Oh,' she breathed. 'So you look like one of them?'

'Yes.'

Her brow wrinkled. 'It must be awful having to pretend to be someone like…that. How do you do it?'

The unexpectedness of the question and the sympathy in her husky voice took his breath away, and for a second he didn't know how to answer. He could already feel himself wanting to smile, to make some dry remark to distance himself from grief inside him. But there was something so unguarded and genuine in her face that he couldn't do it.

So he went with the truth.

'I think about the lives affected by these men,' he said. 'And not just the lives of the people caught up in something like this, but the lives of those who love them. And how if I could even save one person, then that would be worth it.'

Her gaze was liquid, her touch gentle. 'It must be dangerous.'

'I keep myself mostly on the periphery, but it's a fine line. I let them think I'm harmless and not much interested in the business side of their organisation. Plus, I also have the money to manage my own security very well.' The way she was looking at him was making him even more uncomfortable. 'The danger is negligible. It's the people who get caught up with these men who suffer most.'

'Oh, yes, of course. But still. There aren't many men who'd do what you do.'

Her touch was too much, especially in combination with the way she was looking at him, so he shifted his knee, letting her hand slip off. 'I'm not a hero, *mikri alepou*,' he said, his voice rougher than it should have been. 'Some of the things they say about me are correct. If you live with a facade long enough it eventually becomes the truth.'

She folded her hands in her lap and looked down at them, her lashes veiling her gaze. 'I'm sorry,' she murmured. 'I didn't mean to make you uncomfortable.'

Theos, how did she pick up on his emotions so easily? He didn't like that she was able to read him, didn't like it at all. Nor did he like the way his own discomfort had obviously hurt her.

'It's fine,' he said dismissively. 'But I didn't tell you for praise. I told you so you'd understand how important this is and what's at stake.'

'Okay, but…' She hesitated, then went on. 'I know it's none of my business, but can I ask why you're doing this?'

This question at least he'd been expecting.

'You can ask,' he allowed. 'However, my reasons are my own.'

She gave a little nod, but didn't press.

The stewardess came back at that moment, laying out drinks and some snacks. Castor thanked her and picked up his scotch on the rocks, cradling it in his palms, very conscious of Glory's dark eyes on him.

You shouldn't have said anything.

Ah, but that was ridiculous. He'd wanted to tell someone, so he had. What he shouldn't be doing was letting the way she looked at him get under his skin, and he couldn't work out why.

She wasn't anyone special. Just an ordinary woman he happened to have some physical chemistry with, nothing more. Her opinion didn't matter, not at all.

Then Glory said softly, 'This is personal, isn't it?'

He went very still, shock rippling through him, and it was all he could do to keep his gaze level and not snap at her, the beast in him protective of the raw wound in his heart.

She was far too sharp, far too observant, for her own good, because yes, of course this was personal. But Ismena's memory was his to guard and he didn't want to share her, not with anyone.

Castor downed the scotch, then put his glass back on the table in front of him with a click. 'You're right, *mikri alepou*. It *is* none of your business. Now, if you'll excuse me, I have a great deal of work to catch up on.'

Then he got to his feet and without a word he strode down the other end of the plane.

CHAPTER SIX

GLORY STARED AT the deep, rare blue of the Mediterranean as the helicopter circled a perfect little island consisting of dark green trees, white stone buildings, sharp, rocky white stone cliffs and soft, powdery white sand beaches.

Castor's private island.

The beauty of it took her breath away in rather the same way as the man who owned it.

He sat beside her in the helicopter, talking to the pilot in melodic Greek. She had no idea what they were discussing, but the sound of his voice was soothing and she needed soothing, especially after over fifteen hours of travelling.

The journey from LA to Athens had been a long one, despite the luxuries of the private jet. The stewardess had shown Glory to the jet's bedroom—a novelty she hadn't been able to resist trying—but she hadn't slept very well, tossing and turning, and generally not being able to get comfortable.

She wasn't sure why. Probably something to do

with Castor and everything he'd revealed after they'd taken off from LA.

He'd wanted to tell her all those things, that had been clear, and she'd even had the sense that he'd been desperate to talk about them. But only some things, as it turned out.

He'd been uncomfortable with her praise and he definitely had *not* wanted to talk about why taking down the trafficking rings was so important to him.

Not that taking down such things weren't important, she just wanted to know why *he* felt compelled to do so.

Why? What is he to you?

He wasn't anything. Her boss, maybe, if she was thinking of their marriage contract as a job. It was only that what he'd told her about what he was doing had fascinated her and she wanted to know more.

Such as what had led him to put everything he'd worked for—and to get where he was now, he would have had to have worked very hard—at risk. And not only what he'd worked for, but his life too.

What kind of man did that? That question had burned in her mind and the only answer she could come up with was the one thing she'd already noted about him: something was driving him. And it had to be personal somehow given the quiet ferocity in his voice and the glitter in his eyes.

Saving people was *very* important to him.

Not that she was surprised. Despite his anger with her the night at his mansion, she'd known he wasn't the corrupt, jaded womaniser the gossip magazines made him out to be.

He was a knight in shining armour instead.

That's not going to help your obsession with him.

No, it wouldn't, and marrying him wouldn't either. But then she wasn't marrying him for herself, was she? She was doing this for Annabel.

The helicopter descended, heading for the helipad on a flat piece of ground near the most beautiful house. It was constructed of white stone on the side of a cliff, overlooking the sea, and consisted of a series of boxes and terraces on different levels, the terraces bordered by low stone walls. Greenery surrounded it, olive trees and cypresses and all sorts of other trees and shrubs.

She should have been staring out the window at her first glimpse of it amazed, yet her attention kept getting drawn to the man beside her as the helicopter came into land. He wasn't looking at her, his attention out the window, and he was still talking to the pilot. His eyes were hidden behind his sunglasses again, the expression on his face giving no hint as to what he was thinking.

Why had he suddenly ended their conversation on the plane? Was the reason he was doing this painful? Because yes, it had to be, didn't it?

Why are you so curious? What does it matter?

Perhaps it didn't matter. Not that she had the right to demand answers from him anyway and she didn't want to pester him. Annabel used to get irritated with Glory constantly asking her how she was, and she didn't imagine Castor would take it any better than her sister had.

The helicopter came in to land and instantly Castor leapt out. A man was waiting on the helipad and Castor went over to speak to him. They chatted a few moments, then Castor was back, pulling open the door of the helicopter and helping her out.

'I have some things to attend to,' he murmured, his hand strong around hers as she got awkwardly out of the helicopter. 'But Nico here will show you around.'

Then before she could say anything, Castor let her go and strode off down one of the white gravel paths that wound through green lawn and low shrubs towards the house.

Nico, who apparently managed everything, introduced himself, then organised for her bag to be unloaded, picking it up and carrying it himself as he led the way to the house.

It really was a beautiful house, all whitewashed stone, the pretty terraces she'd seen from the air shaded by pergolas overlooking the deep, pristine blue of the ocean beyond. Inside it was white too, with white stone floors and white ceilings. The rooms were large and airy and full of light, with lots of white linen couches and jewel bright cushions scattered here and there. White gauzy curtains fluttered in the warm breeze coming through open windows, and the air was full of the scent of salt and sun and oranges.

The effect was of casual luxury with a rustic touch

that Glory found incredibly appealing. As she did the little touches of art here—folk art sculptures, and paintings and hangings, along with the odd black-and-white photograph that were clearly of the island itself.

Nico showed her to a room in the upper part of the house, with a big bed facing a long line of French doors that opened out onto a private terrace. The room was as white as everywhere else in the villa, as was the en suite bathroom complete with a bath and shower before huge windows that looked out over the sea.

It was incredible, and after Nico had left her alone, with instructions to treat the house as if it were her own, Glory had to pinch herself to make sure she wasn't dreaming.

Used to the LA heat, grime and pollution, and the run-down decor of the apartment she shared with Annabel, being here, where even the air smelled different, was astonishing.

After all the hours spent travelling, she felt tired and gritty-eyed, so she treated herself to a shower, revelling in the huge, white-tiled space, then stood wrapped in a towel in front of her suitcase, pulling a face at her clothing choices. Not that she had many choices. Eventually she pulled out her only skirt—a denim one—along with a clean white T-shirt.

She wasn't sure what to do next and since Castor hadn't given her any instructions, she decided to explore the villa, wandering through a series of interconnecting white rooms and short corridors.

Of Castor himself there was no sign.

Eventually she found herself in one of the smaller rooms where the walls were lined with rustic bookshelves that looked hand carved, the shelves stuffed full of well-thumbed paperbacks in various different genres, plus hardbacks on art and history and science and all kinds of other things.

There were a couple of large, comfortable-looking chairs positioned near the shelves, plus a generous window seat covered in cushions that looked far too inviting to resist. So Glory didn't, curling up in it and gazing out the window at the afternoon sunlight bathing the island in a warm, golden glow.

She should probably call Annabel and tell her she'd arrived safely, but she didn't move, gazing at the view and enjoying being in this beautiful place, in the kind of house that graced expensive home and garden type magazines.

She didn't mean to fall asleep. She was just tired. And she only intended to close her eyes for a couple of moments. So it was very confusing when a deep, male voice said her name softly and she jolted awake, realising that view outside wasn't golden any more but dark, the night sky beyond glittering with stars.

Glory inhaled sharply and turned her head to find Castor standing beside the window seat, looking down at her, his expression unreadable.

'You certainly know how to hide.' There was a faint edge in his voice. 'I've spent the last fifteen minutes searching everywhere for you.'

Heavy-headed with sleep, Glory pushed herself

up from the cushions. 'I'm sorry,' she said thickly. 'I didn't mean to go to sleep.'

He made a tutting sound and reached out, gently pulling away some strands of hair that had been apparently stuck to her cheek. 'Jet lag. Happens to the best of us.'

The intimacy of the movement made her freeze in place, her breath catching, and she found herself staring into his eyes as something deep in them flared into life.

Very slowly, he reached out again, the tips of his fingers brushing her cheek, making everything inside her shiver.

All remaining sleep fled. She felt alive and awake, as if she was standing on the edge of a cliff caught between wanting to hurl herself over it or stay on the safety of her ledge.

For a long moment they stared at each other. Then abruptly he clenched his hand into a fist, the fierce glitter in his eyes extinguished. 'Come, *mikri alepou.*' He turned in the direction of the doorway, his voice casual, betraying nothing. 'Dinner is on the lower terrace and we have some arrangements to discuss.'

Glory tried to will her heartbeat to slow down, her skin tingling from where he'd touched her. Why had he done that? Clearly it hadn't been something he'd enjoyed since he'd then turned away as if she was the one who'd burned him. Like he had the night he'd kissed her.

Then again, had that been heat glittering momentarily in his eyes?

Ah, but she couldn't think about that. If he'd wanted to kiss her again, he would have done so already and he hadn't.

You want him to.

Glory swallowed and ignored that particular thought, just as she ignored the unmistakable lurch of disappointment that followed. Because she had no reason to be disappointed. He hadn't promised her anything but Annabel's IVF treatment and paying off their debt, and a two-week luxury vacation, and that's all.

Pleasant fantasies of kisses and maybe more weren't part of it and neither was wishful thinking.

Sliding off the window seat, she followed him.

The lower terrace was wide, with potted shrubs and various trees in tubs. There was also a long, rustic wooden table with rustic dining chairs and bright cushions on each seat. Food had been laid out—olives and fresh bread, cold meats and salad—along with a bottle of wine and a tall jug full of iced orange juice. Numerous candles in white stone holders had been lit, casting a diffuse and flickering light over the entire terrace.

It looked like a movie set or a scene out of someone else's life. Definitely not her life.

Castor moved over to the table and pulled out a chair, indicating she should sit.

She blushed as she sat down, very conscious of

him standing behind her, tall and powerful and very, very warm.

'That's gentlemanly of you,' she said sincerely. 'For a notorious playboy, I mean.'

Castor pushed her chair in, then moved around the table to sit opposite her, giving her a fleeting glance as he did so. One of those practised smiles turned his mouth. 'I try.' His tone was casual as he reached for a napkin and flicked it over his lap.

'You don't have to do that,' she said without thinking. 'You don't have to pretend. Not with me. Not now I know the truth.'

He went still, his gaze flickering gold beneath his lashes. 'Pretend? Pretend what?'

Should you really have said that?

Why did she keep doing that? Why did she keep talking to him as if she knew him when she didn't? He might have told her his secret on the jet, but only because he wanted her to know what was at stake. It wasn't because he wanted to confide in her specifically. And then she'd pestered him for answers...

She was presuming too much on too little acquaintance.

'It doesn't matter,' she said quickly. 'I shouldn't have said it.'

He leaned back in his chair, his gaze narrowing, his expression opaque. 'But you did say it. So please continue.'

She didn't want to continue, but she also didn't want to argue, so she picked up her own napkin and fussed with it. 'Oh, you know, pretend to smile. Pretend to be charming. Pretend to be the playboy everyone thinks you are.'

'I see.' He gave her a steady and rather unnerving stare. 'And what makes you think I'm pretending?'

'Your s-smile doesn't quite reach your eyes.' Glory fiddled with her napkin. 'It seems kind of… fake. Especially when most of the time with me you don't smile at all.'

He said nothing, his gaze unblinking.

'Like you're doing right now, in fact,' she pointed out.

He stayed quiet.

'Anyway,' she went on quickly, trying to fill up the tense silence. 'All I wanted to say was that you don't have to smile or be charming or…or…anything else with me.'

The tension in the air gathered tighter.

Abruptly Castor reached for the open bottle of wine that stood on the table and with a certain amount of deliberation poured it into two wine glasses.

Glory looked down at the napkin in her lap, smoothing it while her heartbeat raced, anxiety twisting in her stomach.

She shouldn't have said anything. Why had she? She was better at observing people than talking with them and now she'd clearly offended him.

Does it matter if you offend him? He certainly doesn't seem to care if he offends you.

That was true. He had a couple of times and without apology, while she seemed to be apologising to him all the time.

'I'm not the only one who pretends.'

His voice came suddenly from across the table, low and deep, with that edge to it that she thought now was anger.

She looked up from her napkin to find him watching her, making her breath catch.

'Wh-what?'

'You pretend, Glory Albright.' His stare became intent. A predator's stare. 'Don't think I haven't noticed. You seem so shy and so afraid. Stammering like a child whenever you talk to me. Yet I see the way you look at me.' The gold in his eyes glittered as he pushed the wine glass in her direction. 'And I certainly felt it the night you kissed me. There's nothing really shy about you, is there?' He leaned forward slowly, the candlelight leaping and flickering over his fallen-angel beauty. 'You're hungry, *mikri alepou*. You're hungry, just like me.'

Glory was sitting there frozen, her dark eyes fixed on his. Her lush mouth had opened slightly, the pretty freckles dusting her nose standing out under the blush that had risen in her cheeks.

He shouldn't be angry with her. He had no right to be. Yet fury wound through him, hot and raw, coming from a place so deep inside him he hadn't known it was there.

A fury that had begun to climb as he'd spent fifteen minutes searching the villa for her. A fury in direct proportion to the cold thread of worry that had also began to build. Because she didn't seem to be anywhere around and yet no one had seen her leave. He'd ordered Nico to search the grounds while he did another search of the villa, the chill inside him gathering along with his anger.

How dare she make him worry about where she was? And how dare he worry about her at all? Because since when did he care?

The last decade of his life he'd had to cut his emotions off completely or else go mad, and he'd done so successfully. So successfully that sometimes he wondered if he still felt anything at all.

Yet in the space of a week, one ordinary young woman from LA had set alight something inside him and now here he was, frantically searching his villa as if she mattered in any way, and yes, he was furious about it.

And then when he'd gone into one of the smaller rooms he kept as a library, he'd found her lying on the couch fast asleep as if she didn't have a care in the world.

An intense relief had overcome him then, only to be overtaken by an equally intense fury, because why he should be *quite* so relieved he had no idea. She hadn't disappeared inexplicably or been taken by any of the people he was trying to bring down. She'd simply wandered off and fallen asleep on the couch as if he hadn't mobilised the entirety of the villa's staff to look for her.

As if she wasn't lying curled up on the couch with

her hands beneath her chin like a child, pretty russet hair spread over the white linen, the denim miniskirt she wore pulled up to expose rounded thighs and smooth, pale silken skin.

Over the years he'd become so jaded that it took a lot to get him hard. But looking down at her lush feminine curves and her innocence, he felt his fury and relief transform into something burning, that ached, that made him hollow with hunger.

Every part of him had tightened with desire and he'd had to take a step out of the room to control himself. To not simply scoop her up in his arms, carry her straight to his bedroom and punish her for making him angry, for making him worry. For making him feel anything at all, because he didn't like it.

But of course he wasn't going to do that. He'd made his decision not to touch her and he couldn't. Yet the time it took to get himself in hand didn't help his temper, and by the time he'd gone back in to wake her up, he felt as if everything was strangely precarious. As if he was an explorer in unfamiliar territory constantly on the lookout for threats.

Maybe that was why he'd pulled her hair off her cheek and touched her cheekbone. Because he wanted to understand the nature of the threat she presented. Solve the mystery of why she should render his control as brittle as glass.

It had been a mistake though, because even now he could feel the warmth of her skin lingering on his fingertips, as if the very touch of her burned him. Just as it had been a mistake to have this dinner with her, to sit here with her velvety dark eyes focused on him, her deliciously husky voice telling him that now she knew the truth, he didn't have to pretend.

And all he could think about was how great a relief that would be. To have just one person he could be himself with, because he hadn't had that in years. *Theos*, if he'd *ever* had it.

Hungry, he'd said to her and he was. Hungry for someone who saw beneath that mask of his, who saw *him*.

Just as he saw her, no matter how hard she tried to hide it. She wanted him and it was obvious.

'I...I don't know what you mean,' she said thickly, grabbing her wine glass and taking a healthy sip.

He shoved his chair back from the table. 'Then come here and I'll show you.'

What are you doing? You don't want to go down this particular path.

No. This was a game he played with women who knew what they were doing and who liked a challenge just as he did, not with inexperienced innocents like her.

He should be walking away, putting some distance between them, not sitting here staring at her and challenging her to come closer.

Yet he didn't move and he didn't look away. Fury and hunger had him in its grip and he couldn't get free.

You don't want to get free. You want to feel something for the first time in years...

Yes, he did. He couldn't deny it.

Glory put her wine down, her expression turning wary. 'Why? What are you going to do?'

'I think you know exactly what I'm going to do.' He held himself very still, tension gripping every muscle. There was no charm now and all his smiles had disappeared. She'd told him not to pretend and so here he was, not pretending. If she didn't like that after all, well, she knew where the door was.

A long, aching moment passed and then, strangely, concern filled her velvety gaze. 'You're angry with me.'

The sudden change of subject made him catch his breath. 'What?'

'You're angry with me—I can see it in your eyes. Was it something I did?' Her hands moved nervously in her lap, fiddling with her napkin again. 'I shouldn't have fallen asleep, should I? I'm sorry. I was just so tired.'

Theos, did she really think all of this was about anger? Could she not see the desire that burned in his eyes? Or was it simply that she didn't recognise it?

Why would she recognise it? She's had no experience with men, as you know very well.

Castor gritted his teeth. He didn't want to have to explain himself, but it wasn't fair to let her think she'd angered him. Especially when it was obvious that mattered to her since she kept apologising.

'Of course I'm angry with you,' he bit out. 'I'm angry with you for falling asleep and letting me find you all curled up, with your hair across the cushions and your denim skirt up around your thighs. Looking like Sleeping Beauty waiting for your prince to wake you with a kiss.'

'But I—'

'You made me want to do that, Glory. You made me want to kiss you and more. And yes, that made me angry. Because I wasn't going to touch you. Yet all I can think about right now is whether you still want your virginity.' His voice had deepened into a growl and he let it. 'Because if not, I'm quite happy to take it from you right here and now.'

Her eyes went very wide, her mouth opening. Her hands stilled and a tide of colour crept up her neck and over her cheeks, contrasting beautifully with the white of her T-shirt.

'You are?' Her voice had gone hoarse. 'Why? I'm not beautiful. I'm not special. I'm ordinary, remember?'

'I told you that I was wrong about that. And as to why, I don't know. What I do know is that I want you, *mikri alepou*, because you told me that I didn't have to pretend.' He paused, staring into those beautiful eyes of hers. 'So, I'm not pretending.'

Something shifted in her gaze and her mouth closed, her chin suddenly getting a determined slant to it.

She put her napkin down, pushed back her chair and rose to her feet. Then she moved around the table, coming closer to him.

He waited, anticipation tightening inside him, joining his hunger to create something thick and hot. This was a very bad idea and he knew it. He couldn't afford to indulge himself with someone like her, not when she was part of his mission. And certainly not when all he had to offer was a night of pleasure and nothing more.

Glory stopped beside his chair and looked down at him. She smelled of soap and a sweet, musky scent that was all her. It made his mouth water. He wanted to position her between his thighs and make her stand there as he ran his hands up her legs and over the curve of her bottom. Watch that hungry look turn to flame in her eyes and know that it was him she wanted. Really him.

Not the dissipated playboy he pretended to be, but the flawed man he actually was.

The man who couldn't even take care of his own sister.

The thought came and went as Glory laid her fingertips lightly on his hand where it rested on the arm of his chair and said, 'Perhaps you're right. Perhaps I have been pretending. And perhaps I don't want to pretend any more either.'

He stared at her small hand touching his, the heat from her fingertips pinning him there as if she'd run a spear straight through him. Then slowly he lifted his gaze to hers.

Her eyes were so beautiful, dark and full of emotion. Desire burned there, along with fear and excitement and hunger.

And a question she probably didn't even know she was asking.

He knew though, just as he knew the answer.

Castor turned his hand over and closed his fingers around hers. Then he tugged her closer, reaching up to tangle his free hand in her hair, pulling her head down. She didn't resist, her other hand coming down to rest on his shoulder, balancing herself as he tugged her down even further until her mouth brushed over his, his entire being held captive by the softness of her lips on his. He could taste the wine she'd been drinking, both tart and sweet at the same time, which was exactly like her too. Tart and sweet. Sharp and soft. And so warm, so very, very warm…

Her hair fell around him like a curtain and he wanted to bury his face in her curls. But then her mouth opened, her tongue touching his bottom lip, shyly exploring, making electricity crackle the length of his spine, and it abruptly became clear to him that if he didn't stop this he *would* take her virginity here and now.

Do you really have such little control over yourself that you'd ignore doing the responsible thing in favour of what you want instead? And all because of one kiss? Remember what happens when you do that.

A cold thread wound through the heat. Oh, yes, he remembered.

Ismena tugging on his hand, because she wanted him to take her to get ice cream. It was late and he still had a lot of homework to do, and he knew he should refuse. But the girl at the ice cream shop had been flirting with another boy, and he was jealous. He wanted to talk to her, ask her out before this other boy got to her.

So he'd taken Ismena out to get ice cream. And he'd talked to the girl in the ice cream shop. And by the time he'd finally managed to get her number, Ismena had disappeared…

No, he couldn't be so irresponsible again. He couldn't think only of himself. Glory wasn't a little girl and he wasn't fifteen any more, but she was still an innocent and he had the power to hurt her, which made it his job to protect her. Especially when sex was something he could easily get from someone else.

It didn't have to be from her, no matter what his brain insisted on telling him.

Castor released her and pulled away. She looked at him uncertainly, her luscious mouth red from his kiss, and he could feel the heat inside him wanting to break out of the cage he'd put it in.

It was a struggle to control it, but he did.

'Not tonight,' he said quietly, holding her gaze so she could see the decision he'd made in his. 'Not ever. Do you understand?'

Hurt flickered over her face. Then she turned away abruptly, going back to her seat and sitting down, looking down at her plate and saying nothing.

So much for not hurting her.

There was a dull ache in his chest for no reason that he could see so he ignored it. Pain was fleeting and her pain would be fleeting too.

She'd eventually see his refusal as the lucky escape it was and would go on to find another, far more deserving man than he was to gift her virginity to.

Castor reached into his pocket and took out the box he'd put in there earlier that evening, laying it down on the table. 'This is an engagement ring,' he said casually. 'I want you to wear it tomorrow. It's large and expensive and I'd like some pictures of you wearing it.'

He didn't wait to see if she picked the box up.

He got to his feet, turned and walked away.

CHAPTER SEVEN

GLORY DIDN'T SEE him the next morning. Breakfast was served out on the terrace where dinner had been the night before, but there was no sign of Castor when she sat down to eat.

However, there was a note.

Forgive my absence, but I have a few details to attend to this morning.

The marriage ceremony will be conducted tomorrow in the villa's chapel—if you wish to see it, Nico will take you.

You may spend today as you like, but please be advised that I have leaked details of our wedding to the press so there may be some cameras around.

I will join you when I can.

C

Disappointment made her stomach dip, closely followed by a flare of uncharacteristic anger that made her screw the note up into a tight little ball and deposit it next to the ring box she'd left on the table the night before.

He was an ass, that's what he was, and she shouldn't have allowed him to get to her last night. Being honest with him, telling him she didn't want to pretend either, had been a mistake, as had coming around the table to kiss him. She should have shrugged when he'd rejected her, when he'd told her it would never happen between them. She should have told him she didn't care.

Yet she hadn't. She couldn't. She'd never been able to hide her hurt with Annabel either, when her sister had told her she was too busy to talk, too tired to help her with her homework and didn't want to play any of her silly games. That she had more important things to do.

Annabel hadn't had time for Glory's hurts, and since she had enough on her plate already, Glory had decided that it was easier to keep quiet. Easier for her and easier for Annabel too.

So that's what she'd done last night with Castor. She'd gone back to her seat and said nothing, too embarrassed and upset to even look at him. Then he'd simply got up and walked away without a word.

Was it her fault? Had she done something she shouldn't? Misinterpreted him somehow? But then how could she have misinterpreted what he'd said when he'd been very clear about what he'd wanted?

'All I can think about right now is whether you still want your virginity... Because if not, I'm quite happy to take it from you right here and now.'

Her. He'd wanted her. He'd said that.

Except he'd also said, *'Not tonight. Not ever.'*

Glory's hands clenched into fists in her lap, hurt catching inside her.

She didn't understand him. She didn't understand why this was painful either. Because why did she care if he didn't want to sleep with her? What did it matter? She'd told him back in LA that sex wasn't on the table and told herself that she was fine with it. Besides, she hadn't known him very long and he'd never promised her anything.

He just made her feel as if she was ten again, constantly pestering her sister for attention that Annabel was too tired to give.

Too tired because she spent every minute of the day working just so they both had a roof over their heads and food to eat.

She knew she shouldn't let Annabel's small rejections hurt. Her sister hadn't been doing it maliciously. She'd only been trying to look after Glory as best she could. Yet they'd hurt all the same, sitting like a splinter close to Glory's heart, and even now, even as an adult, she could feel that splinter throb inside her.

The only solution was to keep pretending it didn't matter. That this was merely a job she was doing, a vacation she was having. That she didn't want him and he wasn't fascinating and she didn't care at all that he wasn't here.

She left the ring box on the table after she'd finished breakfast, then sent an email to Annabel to let her know she'd arrived safely, since she couldn't bear the thought of actually talking to her.

Once that was accomplished, she settled into the task of doing some serious sightseeing on the island.

It was small, rocky, a little bit wild and utterly beautiful, and Glory loved it. She took a lot of photos on her phone, enjoying the hot Mediterranean sun on the back of her neck, the cloudless blue of the sky and white rocks against the deep turquoise of the sea.

She poked around the chapel where the wedding was going to be the next day; it was tiny and had to be centuries old. It smelled of cool stone and incense, light flooding the small space in front of the altar from the window high above.

Tomorrow, she would be getting married here.

Tomorrow, Castor would be her husband.

The thought shouldn't have made her feel anything since it wasn't even real, yet trepidation turned over inside her as she stared at the altar.

No, she wasn't going to allow herself any nerves. Or if she did, it would only be about what kind of attention it was going to draw, nothing else.

It certainly wasn't going to be about *him*. Because she didn't care about him at all.

She returned to the villa and spent the afternoon by the glorious blue infinity pool, sunning herself in her sagging old swimsuit while she read a book stolen from the library, determined not to notice Castor's absence.

Which turned out to be relatively easy since he remained absent the entire afternoon.

Even after the sun went down and another delicious dinner was served on the terrace, he didn't appear.

Nico, however, arrived with another note.

The ceremony will begin at ten and Nico will escort you to the chapel.

A gown has been laid out for you. Please leave your hair loose.

If you have any questions, Nico will be happy to answer them.

Once again, apologies for my absence.

C

Glory debated on screwing this note up as well and maybe throwing it off the terrace and into the ocean for good measure. But Nico was watching her so she didn't. There was nothing to be gained by being petulant. If he wanted to continue avoiding her, then he could. She certainly wasn't going to go chasing after him. And besides, she didn't care. She really didn't.

If Nico noticed her temper, he made no mention of it, but he glanced at the unopened ring box on the table. Again, though, he didn't say anything.

Rather to her own surprise Glory slept like a log that night, and in the morning woke to find a gown laid over the chair in her room. It was very simple, a shift dress of white silk, cut on the bias to emphasise her curves. She found the simplicity of it beautiful. Beside it was laid a simple wreath of glossy green laurel leaves that presumably she was to wear in her hair.

She showered, then dressed, anger at Castor for his rejection and at herself for caring still burning in her gut, so when two women arrived at her door armed with make-up cases and hair implements ready to help her look presentable, she almost sent them away.

But she'd never had anyone do her make-up, or style her hair, and why should she miss out on something lovely like that, just because Castor Xenakis was being a complete ass? Anyway, she shouldn't be angry. She was here on a beautiful Greek island, having an all-expenses-paid luxury vacation, when she could be back in LA in the grocery store, so really, she should just enjoy it.

Swallowing her anger, Glory let the women fuss around, styling her hair and doing her make-up. And half an hour later, when they were done, Glory barely recognised the woman in the mirror, glowing and fresh-faced and pretty, her dark eyes outlined in gold and looking huge with liberal coats of mascara. Her curls—usually frizzy—were cascading down her back, gleaming and beautiful, the little wreath of laurel and wildflowers laid gently on them.

For the first time in her life, not only did she look beautiful, but she felt beautiful too, and she liked that. She liked that a lot.

It wasn't real, she knew that. She wasn't going to marry the man she loved and who loved her. It was only a job, a bargain she'd made, but she didn't care. Today she felt like a bride and that was enough.

Nico arrived and offered her his arm and together they walked down to the little stone chapel, the sound of helicopters in the air heralding the arrival of the promised media presence.

Glory decided her nerves couldn't deal with cameras so she didn't look up, keeping her attention on the chapel ahead.

Inside it was dark and cool, and smelled of incense and centuries of prayers. Light came down through a narrow window above the altar, shining on the tall figure of a man who was pacing back and forth, clearly restless. The priest was murmuring to him in Greek, while he said nothing.

And despite her best efforts, Glory's chest clenched tight, threads of anger and desire constricting inside her.

Castor was unspeakably gorgeous in perfectly tailored black trousers and a plain black shirt. He wore no tie and though his dress looked casual, it was elegant and simple, setting off his phenomenal good looks to perfection.

The light through the window picked up the gold strands in his dark hair and made his skin gleam, and when he stopped and turned his head, looking to where she stood in the doorway, his eyes glinted pure gold.

She swallowed, clutching onto her bouquet.

He turned to face her, all the restless energy that she'd seen in him as he'd paced before the altar draining away until he stood very still, his gaze focused with complete attention on her.

No one had ever looked at her that way before, as if she was the only thing in the world worth looking at, still less a man like him. As if she was so absorbing he couldn't look away from her in case he missed anything.

A wave of heat swept over her, along with another wash of anger, because how dare he look at her like that, when he'd told her nothing was going to happen between them? How dare he look at her like he wanted her, only to reject her small advances?

She'd always checked herself in the past, not wanting to make things difficult for Annabel, because life had been hard enough for her and she didn't need a little brat for a sister.

However, Castor wasn't Annabel. He might have been a white knight, but he was also rich, privileged, and while he might play these kinds of games with the women who customarily threw themselves at him, he wasn't going to play them with her. She wasn't going to let him.

She might not be one of the people he was trying to save with his mission, and she might be rather plain and her life rather ordinary, but she was still a person. And she had feelings.

And she was tired of being toyed with.

Glory lifted her chin, met Castor's brilliant gaze and slowly walked down the aisle towards him.

He watched her every step, his gaze roving from the wreath in her hair, to her shoulders, to the swell of her breasts, her hips and then down further, before making its way back up again.

She glared at him, angry that he should *still* be looking at her like that, making her heart beat faster and her palms damp where they clutched her bouquet. Angry at the electricity building in the space between them, a snapping, crackling energy that felt like it was bigger than the church they were standing in.

She came to a stop in front of the altar and stared straight into his eyes, more gold now than anything else. There were a million sharp words sitting inside her and she wanted to let them all fly. But to do so would be to let him know he'd hurt her and she didn't want to do that.

So she said nothing, merely stood there giving him what she hoped was a cool look.

The flames in his eyes leapt higher.

'Why weren't you wearing my ring?' he demanded.

It was a stupid thing to say and Castor knew it the second the words were out of his mouth. It betrayed too much. Yet anger was the only emotion that made any sense in that moment.

Anger that the instant she'd appeared in the doorway of the church, the posy he'd had put together clutched in one small hand, her lush, gorgeous figure wrapped in the simple gown of white silk he'd arranged for her to wear, everything he'd told himself about control and denial had gone straight out the window.

As he'd ordered, her glorious hair was loose in an exquisite cloud of curls, prettier than any veil. The flowers and deep green, glossy leaves of the wreath in her hair was the most perfect touch.

She looked young and innocent and heartbreakingly beautiful. Persephone, Goddess of Spring.

Which makes you Hades, dragging her down into the Underworld.

No. He wasn't dragging her anywhere.

He'd been careful to keep away from her the past day, busying himself with organising the details of the wedding and liaising with his PR people to make sure the news being disseminated to the press was exactly what he wanted. Enough of the appearance of reality to make everyone think it really was as real as it looked.

He'd also got in touch with certain contacts as to how the news of his engagement and impending wedding was being received by the leaders of the trafficking ring he was trying to infiltrate. Which was favourably, according to the reports he got back.

He'd hoped that a day would have given him some distance, that his desire for her would become less intense or his control over himself stronger. He had Nico keeping an eye on her, and everything had seemed fine. Then just before he'd walked into the chapel, Nico had mentioned noticing that she hadn't been wearing his engagement ring. And Castor had found himself consumed by the most ridiculous rage.

He couldn't understand why. She wasn't his actual fiancée, and whether she wore the ring or not didn't matter all that much. He'd needed her to wear it for pictures, but that could happen after they were married. It didn't have to be before.

Yet he was still angry.

And it seemed he wasn't the only one, because now she was close he could see fire glowing deep in her dark eyes, and her chin had lifted in a very determined way.

'I wasn't wearing your ring, because I didn't want to,' she said shortly.

Electricity pulsed through him in a hard jolt, the predator in him responding to her challenge.

This is not the time or the place for this argument.

No, and especially not when he was so on edge. Yet he couldn't stop himself. 'You agreed to be my loving fiancée.' He didn't bother to temper his tone. 'And that includes wearing my engagement ring.'

Glory's chin came up higher. 'I might have worn it if that loving fiancé had bothered to talk to me yesterday, but since he didn't, I decided not to wear his stupid ring.'

Ah, so she hadn't liked the distance he'd tried to put between them.

That shouldn't matter.

It shouldn't. But it did.

Her sharp-featured lovely face was flushed, the gold outlining her eyes making them seem ever darker, the anger glowing in them like tiny fires.

And another jolt of electricity hit him hard, his anger twisting, the desire in him deepening.

A mistake to give in to this feeling. A mistake to let himself be at the mercy of it. Yet all he could think of was that it had been far too long since a woman had looked at him with anything but either fear or calculated lust, and Glory's honest anger thrilled him in a way it probably shouldn't have.

He didn't look away from her, holding her gaze with his. 'Give me your hand,' he ordered, reaching into his pocket for the box that contained the engagement ring.

For a second he thought she might disobey, and he half found himself wanting her to purely so he could have the excuse to do something, though what he'd do he wasn't sure. But she only pulled a face and extended her hand.

The priest was looking at them both with some disapproval, but Castor ignored him. He pulled out the ring box and opened it, took the engagement ring from it, discarded the box, then slid the ring onto her finger.

He'd ordered it back in LA and hadn't put too much thought into it, wanting only big and flashy. And flashy it certainly was, a blue diamond set in a platinum band and surrounded by smaller diamonds. It looked too big for her hand and the second he'd put it on, he wanted to take it off, get her something more suitable. Which was ridiculous when none of this was real. It was *all* pretend.

'You don't have to pretend, not with me...'

The memory of her voice from their aborted dinner wound around him and he found himself staring into the velvet darkness of her eyes, seeing the anger burning in them.

You hurt her that night.

Of course he'd hurt her. He knew he had. That's why she was so angry with him now, wasn't it? *Theos*, she had every right to be. He'd told her he wanted her, had kissed her, then had turned around and told her it wouldn't happen, before walking away without even giving her an explanation.

No wonder she was so upset with him.

Regret shifted in his gut, another emotion he never let himself feel these days.

She doesn't need your mission. She doesn't need rescuing. And her hurt is easy enough to heal. You can't fix what happened to Ismena, but you can fix the way you treated Glory. You could give her a wedding night.

The thought hit him like a lightning strike, stealing his breath. No. No, he couldn't. He'd told himself right from the start that he wasn't going to touch her. She was now part of this mission and he couldn't complicate it by sleeping with her.

She wants you. And once you put that ring on her finger, everyone will think you're sleeping with her anyway. If you make the boundaries clear, where's the harm? Besides, you want her too, don't lie to yourself.

The priest coughed, glaring at Castor's silence.

'Begin,' Castor ordered, his voice rough as the

thought dug its claws into him. Because he could, couldn't he? He could give her one night.

It could be…a wedding present even. It wouldn't mean anything. He'd be clear about that.

Glory's chin jutted as the priest began the ceremony, but she said nothing.

Castor couldn't look away. And as the ceremony went on, he watched the blush in her cheeks deepen, the scattering of freckles across her nose looking like fallen stars, and her lush mouth soften. The anger died out of her eyes, something hotter and more intense shifting in the velvety darkness.

His heartbeat thumped in his head and when they took each other's hands to exchange rings, he felt her touch on his skin like a brand.

Then somehow the ceremony was at an end, the priest murmuring that they were husband and wife and that Castor could kiss his bride, and he found himself holding his breath.

He couldn't remember the last time he'd wanted to kiss a woman so badly.

'You don't have to,' Glory said, her cheeks flaming despite the edge in her voice. 'I know you didn't—'

But instinct had him in its grip and he didn't even think, taking her face gently between his palms, tilting her head back and covering her protests with his lips.

She went very still, but he could feel the shiver that shook her.

Her mouth was so soft and she tasted of mint,

along with something sweet. Instinctively he deepened the kiss, because it felt like for the past couple of days he'd been holding himself rigid and yet now, with her lips under his, he could finally relax.

You don't need to pretend with me...

Yet pretending was all he'd been doing for years. Pretending to be someone he'd never wanted to be. Pretending he didn't feel all the emotions he'd tried to cut himself off from. Pretending he was fine with all the things he'd had to do in order to keep up this ridiculous act.

But he'd never been fine and the little girl he'd done it all for was gone. He'd lost her.

Glory wasn't though. She was here and kissing her felt like drinking a cold glass of water after years in the desert. Sheer relief.

He tasted her deeper, sliding his hands lower till they rested at the base of her throat, his fingers caressing her neck. Her skin was smooth and silky and warm, and he wanted to lay her down and discover if she was just as warm and silky everywhere else.

She trembled, then began to kiss him back, shyly at first and then bolder, her tongue exploring his mouth as he'd explored hers, winding his desire tighter and tighter.

She was so responsive. He'd been a fool to deny her. A fool to deny himself. He could teach her so many things, give her so much pleasure...

The priest cleared his throat once again, ostentatiously, and Castor belatedly remembered that he was in a church and he was kissing his new wife in a way that was probably not appropriate.

It was a struggle to drag his mouth from hers, but he managed it, lifting his head and looking down at her. Her face was rosy, her mouth red and soft from the effect of his kiss. Then as he watched, the desire faded from her gaze to be replaced again by a certain challenge.

'You didn't have to force yourself to kiss me,' she said tartly. 'This isn't real, remember?'

The priest was still standing there, but Castor didn't care.

'And if it was?' he asked. 'What if tonight it was all real?'

Surprise rippled over her face. 'What? What are you talking about?'

She is yours now. All yours.

He didn't want to get possessive. That was all too prevalent in the world he lived in, where people were seen as possessions, and he didn't want to turn into that kind of man. But that didn't change the feeling that had him by the throat.

He took her hand tightly in his. 'Come, wife. You and I need to have a little chat.'

'Castor, wait.'

But he didn't want to wait.

He pulled her down the aisle and outside, tugging her in close to shelter her as the sound of helicopters came from overhead. Out in the bay, yachts bobbed, dark figures moving on the decks.

Since the island was private, the media couldn't

gain access to it; not that they needed to when they had telephoto lenses.

Automatically Castor put a possessive hand on Glory's hip, making it clear who she now belonged to, and it wasn't entirely for show this time.

She'd gone rigid, but made no attempt to pull away.

Nico was standing on the church steps, waiting to fulfil his witnessing duties as Castor had specified. It didn't take long to complete the legalities. Five minutes later Castor said, 'My wife and I are going back to the villa.' He gave his manager a very direct look. 'Alone.'

He didn't wait for Nico's response, merely firmed his grip on Glory and urged her along the white gravel path back up to the villa.

'Castor, what are you doing?' She sounded breathless. 'I know you didn't want to kiss me, so why did you?'

But he didn't want to have this discussion here, not out in the open with unseen cameras trained on them, so he didn't reply, hurrying her along the path lined with olive trees and up through some terraces, until finally they were safely back inside the villa.

Glory was glaring at him as he shut the door of the living room firmly behind them. She still had the posy in one hand, a handful of white silk in the other since the gown was long and she had to lift the hem. The wreath in her hair was slightly askew, curls drifting over her shoulders, and he wanted to grab her, undress her, scatter the flowers everywhere around them and lay her down on the petals like the virgin sacrifice she was.

'What is this all about, Castor?' she demanded, before he could speak. 'You just walked out the night before last without even a word, then you spent the whole of yesterday avoiding me, sending me ridiculous notes—'

'Yes.' He took a couple of paces towards her, itching to take her in his arms. 'You're right, they were ridiculous. And yes, I was avoiding you.'

She blinked, obviously taken aback. 'Why?'

'I think you know why.' He took another few steps, getting closer. 'You offered me something precious and I refused you. Then I walked out without explanation. I shouldn't have.'

She gave him a wary look, but didn't move as he came closer still. 'No, you shouldn't have. Especially considering you kissed me back. I thought…I thought I did something wrong.'

'You didn't do anything wrong.' He was so close now, inches away from her, and he didn't hesitate, reaching for her, his hands settling on her hips and drawing her up against him.

She gasped, her bouquet dropping onto the floor as she lifted her hands to his chest, her palms pressing against him, holding him away. 'What are you doing?'

The heat of her body seeped through the thin silk of her wedding gown and into his palms like the promise of a fire on a cold, dark night, and he wanted to sit in front of it, let it warm him right through.

'What am I doing?' He eased her closer, fitting her softness against all the hard, aching parts of him. 'I'm doing what I should have done that night instead of walking away.' He lifted one hand and slid his fingers into her hair, cupping the back of her head. Then he held her still as he bent and kissed her again.

She made a soft sound, the pressure of her palms increasing on his chest, but it wasn't to push him away. And when he pushed his tongue into her mouth, her fingers curled in his shirt as if she wanted to pull him closer.

He should talk, explain himself, but he was tired of talking. He was tired of denial. It felt like he'd been denying himself for years, and finally, now he had something he really wanted here in his hands, he couldn't deny himself any more.

He kissed her deeper, letting hunger stretch out inside him, exploring the sweetness of her mouth with care before turning the kiss hotter, letting it build until there was a fever to it, and she was trembling against him, gripping him tightly as if she needed to hold onto him to stop herself from falling.

It was only then that he lifted his head, not hiding the hunger in his eyes, letting her see it.

She was breathing very fast, her make-up smudged, the darkness of her eyes thick and soft as midnight in midsummer. 'C-Castor...I don't understand,' she said, all breathless and husky. 'I thought... you said it would...n-never happen.'

'I know what I said.' His hand was still in her hair, chestnut curls wound around his fingers, but his thumb was free and he used it to trace a line across the silky skin of her cheekbone. 'But I decided I was wrong. I want you, *mikri alepou*. And I want to give you a wedding night.'

Her mouth opened, then shut. 'A…wedding night?'

'Yes.' He ran his thumb over her cheek, down to the corner of her mouth, tracing the line of her lower lip. 'I can only offer you one night, that's all. But if you want it, all you need to do is say yes.'

The pulse at the base of her pretty throat was beating very fast, the expression on her face slightly dazed. She felt so good against him and the musky, sweet scent of her was making his mouth water.

'You made me so angry,' she whispered. 'You… hurt me.'

Regret pulled tight inside him. 'I'm sorry. I was… trying to protect you. You're too young and you're too innocent, and you shouldn't be getting tangled up with a man like me.' He bent and brushed his mouth over hers, feeling the heat of her stoke the flames already burning inside him. 'I didn't want to complicate this and I thought distance would be better.'

'No.' She leaned into him, trying to follow his mouth, her eyes half closed. 'No, distance is not better.' Her lashes lifted and abruptly he was lost in the warm sooty darkness of her eyes once again. 'I might be inexperienced, but you don't have to treat me like a child. I know what you can and can't give me, and I'm okay with that.'

'Glory, I—'

She lifted a hand and pressed a finger against his

mouth, the touch stealing the words straight out of his head. 'If you want my virginity, Castor Xenakis, then stop talking and take it.'

CHAPTER EIGHT

GLORY SHIVERED AS gold fire ignited in Castor's eyes and her whole body gathered tight in preparation for another of those soul-destroying kisses.

But he didn't bend his head. Instead his grip on her changed and she was turned around so her back was to him. Then she felt the tug on the zip of her gown, the fabric loosening around her as he drew it down.

He touched the top of her spine gently before his fingers began a long, slow stroke down her exposed back.

She caught her breath. She wasn't sure exactly why he'd changed his mind about her, but she definitely wasn't going to argue with him.

If he wanted to give her a wedding night, then she was going to take it.

Is that really all you want from him?

But she didn't want to think about that so she ignored the thought, concentrating instead on the touch of Castor's fingers on her bare skin as he slid them beneath the straps of her gown, easing the fabric from her shoulders, leaving her standing in a puddle of white silk, wearing only the lacy underwear she'd put on that morning.

He pulled her close, her back against his front, his mouth nuzzling the soft curve of her shoulder and the tender place where it met her neck, nipping her there.

She gasped as electric shocks of pleasure jolted her, all her senses spinning at the heat of his hard body pressed to hers and the warm spice of his aftershave surrounding her.

It felt so good she couldn't breathe. She arched against him, tilting her head back and exposing her throat to him in wordless invitation. Which he took, his teeth against her skin, biting her gently, before soothing the nip with a soft rain of kisses.

Oh, she had no idea it would be like this. How good it felt to be held, to have a man's mouth on her skin and his tall, muscular body behind her, a delicious kind of threat that both excited her even as it scared her.

Just any man?

No, not just any man.

'Castor...'

His name was both a prayer and a demand for more and he answered it, flicking her bra open, pulling the delicate fabric away to leave her breasts bare, then sliding his large, strong hands around to cup them in his palms.

Heat swept through her, along with the most delicious pleasure, and she groaned, arching into his hands, wanting more. Part of her was horrified at how demanding she was being, but the rest of her simply didn't care.

She'd never been wanted like this before, and even though she'd been angry, she'd also loved the way he'd looked at her in the church. And then the way he'd pulled her in close on the way up to the villa, as if he wanted her all to himself.

It made her feel special and she hadn't realised quite how much she'd wanted to be special to someone. Special and not a burden the way she was with Annabel.

But Annabel doesn't get to fly to Greece or be wanted by a beautiful billionaire...

Glory pushed the thought away. No, Annabel was getting her dream, so why couldn't Glory have this for herself? She'd intended to do so back in LA that night in Castor's mansion after all. And besides, it was only a night, nothing more.

Castor's fingers tightened, his thumbs finding her nipples, circling them gently before giving each a little pinch, sending shock waves of pleasure through her, scattering all her doubts.

No one had ever made her feel the way he did and even if this would all end in heartache for her, she wasn't going to regret this. How could she? If she wanted to lose her virginity to someone, she couldn't have asked for a better man to lose it to.

His mouth was warm and seductive on her neck, his body against her back a wall of heat, hard muscle and power. She liked how protected she felt standing right here in his arms, how insulated against anything that would hurt her. It made her aware of how lonely her life had been up till now and how she hadn't known how much she'd wanted someone to hold her until he'd taken her in his arms.

There had only ever been her sister and all the sacrifices Annabel had had to make for her. Everything had a price, and that included love.

But not this. This was free. There was no guilt attached. It was just pleasure and so she'd take it.

Glory arched back against him, wanting more, wanting his hands on her, wanting to lose herself in his touch and in the thrill of being desired by someone like him.

He stroked her breasts gently once more before his hands slid down to her hips and he was easing down the panties she wore, undressing her completely.

She felt no embarrassment, no need to cover herself, not when it was so obvious how much he wanted her, and so when he turned her in his arms to look at her, she met his gaze without shame.

He didn't speak, but that look in his eyes told her everything she needed to know, and when he lifted her in his arms and carried her to the couch, she could see the need in him.

'I want you, Castor,' she heard herself say as he laid her down. 'I want you so much.' She reached up to touch his cheek, loving the feel of his hot skin and the prickle of his whiskers.

He turned his head, kissing her fingertips before straightening, his hands going to the buttons of his shirt and beginning to undo it.

Glory pushed herself up, suddenly dry-mouthed and desperate to touch him, but too shy to ask.

He seemed to know what she wanted though, because he paused, his golden gaze catching hers. 'Would you like to do the honours?' he asked softly, his hands dropping away from the buttons.

She nodded jerkily, coming off the couch to stand before him, reaching for the buttons of his shirt and fumbling a little with them. But he helped her and slowly he was revealed, the black cotton parting to reveal golden skin and hard, carved muscle.

Her hands shook as she touched him reverently, because he was a work of art and works of art should be worshipped.

'Ah, *mikri alepou…*' His voice had got deep, the rough velvet becoming gravel as she ran her fingertips over his chest, tracing the lines of his pectorals before moving downward to the hard corrugations of his abs. 'You will be the death of me.'

But he didn't stop her as she pushed his shirt from his broad shoulders or when she rose on her toes and pressed her mouth to his throat, tasting salt and musk and the essential flavour that was all him. It was only when her hands went to the buttons on his trousers and she undid them, sliding her fingers inside and finding the smooth hot skin of the hardest part of him, that he gave a rough curse in Greek and then moved suddenly.

And then she was on her back once more on the couch, pressed against the seat cushions by his naked body, surrounded by the scent of warm spice, the oiled silk of his skin moving against hers.

He was between her thighs, leaning over her, his hands on either side of her head, his hot gaze burning down into hers. 'You deserve better than this,' he said. 'You deserve time, but I'll make it up to you, I promise.'

She didn't know what he was talking about, mainly because she didn't want time. What she wanted was more of this pleasure, more of his touch, more his kisses, just…more.

And he gave it to her, his hand sliding beneath her hips and lifting her, then a deep, hard thrust that had her crying out. There was pain, but it wasn't bad, a fleeting hurt and then a feeling of fullness, of completeness.

He stilled deep inside her, looking down into her eyes, murmuring something soft in Greek that she didn't understand.

But she thought she knew, so she took a breath, adjusted herself to the feel of him inside her, to the rightness of it, then reached for him, bringing his mouth down to hers.

The kiss was deep and intense, a feverish, hungry kiss, turning even hungrier as he began to move, setting a rhythm that had her trembling and shuddering with pleasure.

She hadn't known it was possible to feel this way, to be so consumed by another person that she thought she might die if he didn't shift his hips in just that way, giving her the most exquisite source of friction that made her gasp in delight. If he didn't bite her bottom lip, or trail kisses down her throat, or slide so deep inside her he made pleasure echo through her entire being.

His arms came around her, his mouth becoming more demanding, the rhythm faster, harder, the pleasure pulling tight until it felt like she was going to snap like a rubber band stretched too far.

She writhed in his arms, gasping, and then his hand was between her thighs, stroking the most sensitive part of her, and everything abruptly came apart and she called his name, lost beneath the flood of an almost unbearable ecstasy. She was only dimly aware of his sudden, sharp movement and then the rough sound of his groan as he chased his own climax, before his body came down on hers.

She didn't mind, floating pleasantly in the aftermath, the hot weight of him like an anchor that kept her tethered and not floating away to be lost in the currents.

Then she felt him cupping her cheek and she realised her eyes were closed, so she opened them, looking straight up into his beautiful face.

His expression was warm, but not the forced, brittle charm she'd seen that night of the party. This was natural, his amber gaze smoky with heat. 'Are you okay? Nothing too sore?'

His body was a hot weight on her, pinning her to the couch, and while there were a few…tender spots, she'd never felt better in her entire life. 'Yes, I'm okay. No, wait.' She smiled. 'I'm better than okay. I think I might even be great.'

His thumb moved idly across her cheekbone in a caressing movement, and though he didn't smile back, his gaze had softened.

She liked the way he was looking at her, with warmth and a certain tenderness, as if her well-being was important to him. As if *she* was important to him and not a burden he had to carry.

'What about you?' she asked, stroking the broad plane of his chest. 'Are you okay?'

He did smile then and it made her feel as if she'd won a prize. 'Oh, you don't need to worry about me, *mikri alepou.*' His thumb moved down, along the line of her jaw. 'Phenomenal doesn't even being to cover it.'

She flushed with pleasure, then a sudden doubt gripped her. 'But if sex is always like that—'

'Sex is never like that,' he interrupted, his smile vanishing, leaving behind it the burning ferocity that lay at the heart of him. 'At least it's never been like that for me.'

Glory stared at him in surprise, because that surely couldn't be right. He was very experienced, had had a lot of women, so why would being with her be so different?

'Why not?' she asked. 'I'm not that special, Castor. I'm just an ordinary woman—'

'You're not an ordinary woman.' The gold in his eyes glinted brighter. 'Because if you were, you wouldn't drive me as mad as you do. I wouldn't be

thinking about you, or trying to resist you, or arguing with you about wearing my ring in front of the
altar. And I certainly wouldn't be lying naked with
you on the couch and thinking about how I'd love
to make you scream again, except louder this time.'
He brushed his mouth over hers, nipping at her bottom lip. 'Glory, you're not ordinary, you're *ex*traordinary, understand?'

When he looked at her like that, she did feel extraordinary. Not a simple checkout girl in a grocery
store, the burden her sister had to bear, but someone
beautiful and mysterious. Someone special.

She blushed. 'I don't feel it sometimes.'

He gave her another nip. 'Well, I hope you're feeling it now, because it's true.'

Glory shuddered in delight, then put her hands on
his broad shoulders, stroking his skin as she looked
up into his face. 'Yes, I do feel it. You make me feel
it, Castor.'

'I'm glad, *mikri alepou*.' He stared down at her
for a long moment, the fierce currents of his emotions shifting in his eyes. Then he turned his head
in the direction of the windows, as if he'd heard a
noise, the lines of his beautiful face hardening. 'A
little privacy, I think.'

He pushed himself off the couch and strode over
to the windows, apparently not caring that he was
naked. He grabbed the curtains and jerked them
closed, before turning and coming back to the couch.

Then he settled himself back on top of her, making her breath catch at the feel of his bare skin slid-

ing against hers. 'There now,' he murmured. 'Where were we? Oh, yes…about here, I think…' He bent his head, nuzzling at the base of her throat, his lips brushing over her skin.

Glory shut her eyes and drew in a shaky breath, heat rippling throughout her entire body. 'Did you hear something?'

'No.' His breath ghosted over her skin as he moved lower, trailing kisses over her collarbones. 'Just keeping out any eavesdroppers.'

Glory wanted to ask him why he thought there'd be any eavesdroppers on a private island, especially when he'd told his staff to absent themselves, but then his lips closed around the aching tip of her nipple, and her thoughts fractured, everything lost but for the exquisite pressure of his mouth and the sparks of pleasure lighting her up inside.

She forgot about eavesdroppers. Forgot about how this wasn't real. She forgot about everything but him and his mouth on her body and his hands on her skin, him inside her, moving hard and deep and fierce, showing her how good he could make her feel.

He was amazing. She'd never experienced anything like him in her entire life.

Afterwards, when their hunger had been sated for the time being, he picked her up and carried her up to his bedroom and the huge, white-tiled shower in the adjoining bathroom, where he washed her gently and with a care that brought tears to her eyes.

She hadn't been looked after like this since she was a child, and even then, looking into Annabel's tired face every day, she knew what a burden taking care of her was. Even worse that Annabel *had* to do it because Glory was her sister.

But Castor didn't have to. There was no obligation on him at all. He was doing it because he wanted to, and while she made a cursory protest, he ignored it so she gave up, letting herself enjoy it and not feel guilty.

After they'd got out of the shower, he insisted on drying her, kneeling in front of her with a soft white towel and wiping the moisture from her skin. She watched him as he did so, wondering why he was doing it and what he was getting from it, because he was getting something, that was clear.

'You like taking care of people, don't you?' she asked, the question escaping before she could think better of it.

He didn't look at her, intent on what he was doing. 'What makes you say that?'

'I mean, you put food on my plate when we ate, and then you insisted on washing me and now you're drying me. I can do all of those things myself.'

His hand ran down her calf to her heel, urging her foot up, and she had to put her hands on his broad shoulders to keep her balance. 'I know you can.' He held her foot in his hand and began to dry it, his touch making her shiver. 'But I want to do it.'

'Why?' His skin was hot underneath her hands, his muscles tensing and relaxing with his movements. He was so very strong—she could feel the power in him—yet he touched her carefully and with great gentleness. It made her heart feel tender for reasons she didn't understand. 'What do you get out of it?'

'I think you know what I get out of it.' He put her foot down, then reached for the other one, glancing up at her briefly, wickedness glowing in his eyes. 'Sex, of course.'

He sounded flippant, but the muscles beneath her hands were rock hard with tension. He didn't like this particular topic of conversation, did he?

Perhaps she shouldn't push it, make a nuisance of herself. Then again, she kind of wanted to know.

'That would make sense if we hadn't had sex,' she said. 'But we have. Yet you're still taking care of me like this, so…why?'

He finished with her foot, releasing it, then rising to his full height, wrapping the towel around her as if she was a child. 'You don't like it?' He lifted a brow. 'Shall I stop?'

Clearly he wasn't going to make this easy for her.

Glory frowned. 'You shouldn't answer a perfectly valid question with another question.'

He smiled faintly, putting a thumb between her brows and smoothing it like he had done earlier downstairs. 'You shouldn't frown like that. You'll get wrinkles.'

'I don't care about wrinkles and next you'll be telling me I should smile more.'

'You should.' He bent and picked her up in his arms, turning to the door and walking through it. 'You have a beautiful smile.' He glanced down, brandy-coloured gaze holding hers. 'I would like to make you smile more.'

Glory's chest went tight as some strange, powerful feeling coiled uncomfortably inside her.

'You do, Castor,' she murmured, touching the smooth skin of his chest. 'And I'd like to do the same for you too.' She stroked him. 'But I'm not sure I can. You hardly ever smile at me.'

His expression shifted, the fierce glow in his eyes becoming softer. 'Didn't you tell me that I didn't have to pretend with you? Well, I don't, *mikri alepou*. All that charm is what I do for them.'

She'd already worked that out for herself, but she liked that he'd told her that anyway. 'So, what? You're actually a pretty serious person, then?'

His expression shifted again, a bleak look crossing his face that made everything inside her clench tight. But then he glanced away, the bleakness vanishing as quickly as it had come. 'Well, now, that's for me to know and you to find out.'

He doesn't smile, not at all. Because something terrible happened to him.

The thought was instant and cold, like ice in her veins, and worse, it felt like the truth. It had to be, didn't it? Something was driving him to put himself at risk the way he did, and she'd already sensed it was personal.

And it could only be something terrible. Why would he choose to infiltrate those trafficking rings? Why pretend to be one of those awful people for nothing?

You can't ask him. You don't have the right.

No, it wasn't any of her business. She might be his wife and he might have decided to give her a wedding night, but it was only sex. It wasn't her place to demand his secrets, no matter how badly she wanted them.

She stayed silent as he carried her into the bedroom, setting her down on the huge bed, before turning and going over to a dresser that stood against one wall.

She stared at him as he pulled something out of a drawer, trying to distract herself from the sharp edge of worry that sat inside her, and his body was certainly a good distraction. Tanned, golden skin and carved muscle, with a narrow waist and long powerful legs.

Oh, she could stare at him all day.

'Y-you're quite extraordinary too,' she said at last, trying break the thick silence. 'I don't know if anyone's ever told you that, but it's true.'

Castor turned around, holding something in his hand. He didn't smile, but the flickering gold in his eyes leapt. 'What makes you say that?' He came back over to where she sat and pulled the towel carefully away from her. Goosebumps prickled all of her skin as he looked down at her, all his attention very focused.

'What you're doing,' she said quietly. 'Your... mission. You're helping people regardless of the cost to yourself and that...that's extraordinary.'

He reached out, touching her face gently. 'You

would do the same in my place, I think. Because you want to help people too, don't you? Your sister, for example. There aren't many people who'd gatecrash a party in order to sell their virginity to a complete stranger, and all for someone else's benefit.'

Glory lifted a shoulder. 'Annabel and I lost our parents when we were young and she ended up having to look after me. She had to make a lot of sacrifices and then she got breast cancer and her fertility was affected. So I...just wanted to do something to help her.'

'Lift your arms for me,' he murmured. She did so, and he shook out the shirt of soft dark blue linen that he was holding and slid her outstretched arms into the sleeves. 'How old were you when you lost your parents?'

He wasn't looking at her, which somehow made it easier to talk about, even though she would have sworn it wasn't actually hard. 'Ten.' She swallowed. 'Annabel was eighteen.'

'That must have been hard.' He pulled the shirt up around her shoulders, his attention falling to the buttons.

The linen felt silky against her skin and it smelled of him. She found it comforting. 'Yes. It was. And certainly for her.'

'I see.' He began to do up the buttons on the shirt. 'But not for you?'

She'd never spoken about it with anyone—mainly because no one had asked—and she really didn't like talking about it, but for some reason, with him, the words were easy to say. 'I missed my parents, of course. But it was Annabel who had to do the hard stuff. She dropped out of school to work so we had enough money to live on.'

Castor said nothing, still apparently involved in doing up the last couple of buttons.

But his silence felt…welcoming somehow, as if he was giving her space in which to speak.

'She had to make lots of sacrifices for me,' Glory went on, because now she'd started, it seemed she couldn't stop. 'She had to give up her education so we could survive. And then she got cancer, which didn't seem fair after everything she'd sacrificed, because she really wanted a family.'

Annabel, so tired after a full day working at the supermarket checkout.

Annabel, changing into her waitress uniform for her second job at the café, still looking exhausted.

Annabel, crying at night after she'd thought Glory had gone to sleep.

But Glory hadn't gone to sleep. She'd heard her sister weeping, heard her talking to a friend on the phone about how it was so hard and how she didn't know how she was going to keep Glory fed and clothed or give her the opportunities she deserved.

Glory, whose presence had made Annabel's life such a misery.

'It wasn't easy for an eighteen-year-old to bring up a kid,' Glory said softly, keeping her hands in her lap. 'And I was impulsive and a bit of a dreamer. I tried to make thing easier for her by behaving myself, doing my homework and staying quiet, and not being too demanding. But...' She stopped, feeling vulnerable all of a sudden. She'd never said any of this stuff out loud before and it was oddly exposing.

A finger caught her beneath the chin, gently tilting her head back so she had to meet his gaze. 'But?' he prompted.

You can tell him. You can tell him anything.

She didn't know where the thought came from, but instinctively she knew it was true. And she'd told him half of it anyway...

'But I knew I was a burden to her all the same,' she said starkly. 'It didn't matter how good I was or how quiet, my very existence was the issue. She never said anything to me and she never complained, but I could hear her crying at night. She was always so tired, always so worried about money. Annabel didn't choose me. I wasn't her child, only her little sister. She got stuck with me. She had to make all these sacrifices for me and then she got cancer and I...' Glory stopped, the secret fear she'd never actually spoken of suddenly right there in her mouth.

'You what?' Castor prompted gently.

And she found herself saying, 'I wonder sometimes if her life would have been easier if I hadn't been in it.'

Glory's eyes were full of unshed tears, making them look even more liquid and dark, and Castor felt a primitive, fierce emotion gather inside him in response. He knew what it was like not to have his little sister in his life, he lived it every day, and it had damn near ruined him.

'No,' he said fiercely, gripping her. 'No, it would *not* be easier if you hadn't been in it. Why on earth would you think that?'

Glory tried to pull away, but he didn't release her. Instead her lashes fell, veiling her gaze. 'She didn't choose me. I wasn't her kid. I was only her sister. I wasn't anyone special. I didn't do anything to—'

'Glory,' he cut her off roughly. 'You didn't have to do anything. You were her sister, that's enough.'

Her lashes rose, droplets of tears sparkling on the ends. Yet a certain anger glowed there too along with the pain. 'How would you know? You weren't there and you don't know Annabel. You didn't see how tired she was. How she had to drop out of school to look after me. You didn't hear her crying at night or talking to a friend about how she didn't know how she was going to feed us for the next week. And you weren't there when she got sick, and all I could think about was how maybe her getting sick was my fault. If she hadn't worked herself into the ground trying to look after me, she might not have got cancer, and then she might have had the baby—'

Castor lifted his thumb and pressed it against her soft mouth, stopping the flood of words. He hadn't wanted to talk about Ismena, but the pain in Glory's eyes was too much to bear. He hated her thinking she was a burden, that somehow she wasn't the special woman he knew her to be. Warm and empathetic and giving. No wonder Annabel had made sacrifices for her. Who wouldn't?

Ismena had been the same, and he would have moved mountains for her.

'I had a little sister,' he said, the words coming out hoarse. 'And I often had to look after her. She was never a burden and I never regretted even a single moment of the things I had to do for her.'

Glory's eyes widened. Then she asked, her lips moving against his thumb, 'You had a sister?'

He shouldn't have said anything, but it was too late. He'd only wanted to make her feel better, nothing more, yet now he'd mentioned Ismena, he couldn't pretend he hadn't.

She was such a precious memory and he guarded her fiercely even now.

You want Glory to know what you're really like? How you were supposed to be the responsible older brother? How you were supposed to be keeping an eye on her?

The thought was barbed wire winding around his heart, cutting into him, the guilt eating away at him.

Yes, she should know. She should understand that the good side she'd apparently seen in him was a lie. That he wasn't any kind of hero. Just a selfish man who'd put his own feelings ahead of taking care of his little sister.

He let her go and straightened, staring down at her.

Wearing nothing but his shirt, with her hair lying in damp, gleaming curls down her back, she looked stunningly beautiful. And it satisfied him on some deep level that she was wearing something of his. It made him feel territorial and possessive, feelings he should have buried the day Ismena disappeared.

Apparently though, he hadn't buried those feelings deep enough.

You can't let them rule you, not again.

Oh, he wouldn't. But one night he'd allow himself and so he'd give them free rein. Tomorrow he'd bury them back in the grave he'd put them in and this time he'd make sure they stayed buried.

'I had a little sister,' he said at last. 'Or maybe I still do, I don't know. Ismena disappeared twenty years ago.'

A crease appeared between Glory's brows, but this time he didn't smooth it away. 'What happened?'

'My father was never in the picture so my mother brought us up. We lived in Athens, in a tenement. My mother worked a lot so I ended up looking after Ismena most of the time. I was…fifteen, Ismena was eight.' He found himself fixating on one of the buttons of the shirt she was wearing. It wasn't in the buttonhole properly so he adjusted it. 'There was an ice cream shop nearby with a girl behind the counter that I was interested in. Another boy was also interested in her and I wanted to ask her out before this other boy did, so that night I told Ismena I'd take her out for ice cream.' His voice got rougher. 'There was a pet shop next door to the ice cream place and they had some new kittens, and Ismena wanted to look at them. So I told her she could while I got the ice cream, because I didn't want her listening in to my conversation. I was only gone a minute, but when I got back, Ismena wasn't there.'

A terrible sympathy stole over Glory's face, and he knew all at once that if she spoke he wouldn't be able to bear it. He'd have to turn around and walk out. Because sympathy was something he didn't deserve.

But she didn't say a word. Instead she reached out and took his hand.

There was warmth in her fingers and a strength he hadn't expected, and he found himself holding her small hand in his.

He didn't want to keep admitting to all the things he'd failed to do, yet her touch seemed to lend him some of that strength, because he found himself going on. 'I searched all night. I searched everywhere. And I did the next day and the next, and the next. I searched for months. I searched for years. But...I never found her. There was a trafficking ring operating in the area at the time and the general consensus was that she'd been taken.'

'Is that—?' Glory stopped and cleared her throat, her fingers tightening around his. 'Is that why you're infiltrating those traffickers?'

It was a simple question and because it had a simple answer, he answered it. 'Yes. My mother and I were poor back then, completely disposable, and the police didn't do a thing to help us. So I swore I'd become rich and powerful enough that I'd find Ismena myself.' He turned her hand over in his, stroking the back of it with his thumb. 'I was single-minded in my intentions. I made myself rich and powerful. And even though I haven't managed to find Ismena, I'll take down these goddamn traffickers if it's the last thing I do.'

The words hung in the space between them and he couldn't say there wasn't a small measure of relief at being able to say her name to another person. At having the acknowledgement that she existed.

'Castor,' Glory said carefully. 'How long have you been searching for her?'

He looked down at their linked hands, her narrow, delicate fingers folded between his longer, larger ones. 'Since she disappeared,' he said. 'Twenty years, though I've only been infiltrating the trafficking rings for ten.'

Theos. Had it really been that long? Then again, searching for her had consumed his life to the point where he couldn't remember *not* searching for her. Couldn't remember a time when she hadn't been the first thing he thought of when he woke up and the last thing he thought of when he went to sleep.

She consumed his every waking thought. He didn't have room for anything else.

Glory was quiet. Then abruptly, she brought his hand to her mouth, kissing it, before releasing it and slipping off the bed to kneel at his feet.

He looked down at her, allowing himself this view because she was so pretty kneeling there with her hair all around her and her big dark eyes gazing up into his.

'I want to give you something,' she said. 'A wedding present of my own. Will you let me?'

He'd had many women kneel at his feet like this, but for some reason with Glory it was different. She wasn't looking at him like he was Castor Xenakis, playboy, but as if he was just Castor. A man she wanted. A man she even might care about.

You don't want her caring for you.

He didn't, but he was done walking away from her. He wasn't going to hurt her again and definitely not when she was offering herself to him.

'What kind of wedding present?' He reached down and took a lock of her hair, curling it around his fingers, liking the feel of it on his skin. Liking her at his feet too, as if she was his. As if she belonged to him.

You can't start thinking like that. She can't be yours. You can't let her matter, you know this.

Oh, he knew and normally he'd never permit himself such emotions. But he'd allowed himself this night with her, which meant he could allow himself the feelings that went with them, surely?

Is a night enough?

Glory put one hand on his thigh, the other sliding up to grip the rapidly hardening length of his sex. The feel of her fingers closing around his hot flesh, soft and cool, stole the breath from his lungs.

'This kind,' she murmured, squeezing him lightly. 'A night to forget.'

Shock rippled through him that she'd somehow

guessed how consumed he was, that she saw what he didn't even know he needed himself.

Because yes, that's exactly what he wanted. A night to forget. A night where he didn't think of Ismena at all.

He wound the lock of hair tighter around his finger. 'Yes. You can try, *mikri alepou*. If you think you can.'

It was a challenge to her, he knew that, and he could see something light up in her dark eyes, the fierce part of her meeting his.

She didn't say anything, but when she put her mouth on him, he felt himself catch fire. Because if anyone could help him forget it was her, and what was more, he wanted her to.

He gripped her hair tighter as the heat of her mouth took him and even though she was inexperienced and this wasn't new to him, feeling her lips against his skin made him groan.

It felt new. It felt like a wonder, a delight he hadn't expected, especially when he showed her what he liked and she set to doing it with a will.

He hadn't thought it was possible, but in the end she did it.

She made him forget, and for a few, blissful moments, he was free.

And afterwards, when he picked her up and had her back on the bed where she belonged, beneath him, he'd already decided: no, one night wasn't going to be enough.

He wanted more.

CHAPTER NINE

Two weeks later, Glory stood in front of the ornate, full-length mirror in the bedroom of Castor's Parisian mansion and smoothed her hands down her sides nervously.

Castor was taking her to a special gala at the Musée d'Orsay, and among all the things he'd bought for her over the past couple of weeks was the most beautiful formal gown. She'd been wary of putting on something so terrifyingly expensive, some part of her worried she'd tear it or ruin it, or somehow look awful in it.

But she didn't look awful in it. She looked... beautiful. She even felt beautiful.

Glory smiled at herself in the mirror.

He's going to love it. He's especially going to love taking it off.

A delicious shiver worked its way down her spine.

Two weeks of being in Castor's bed had certainly taught her many things, including how much he loved undressing her. Slowly and with care, paying meticulous attention to detail, running his fingers over every inch of her body. Treating her as if she was a precious object.

It made her feel worshipped.

He'd made her feel worshipped these whole two weeks, right from the moment she'd woken up in his bed the morning after their wedding.

He'd rolled over, pinned her to the bed, then said, 'How would you feel, *mikri alepou*, about a proper honeymoon?'

That he'd changed his mind about only offering her one night was obvious, and part of her had wanted to ask him why. But after what he'd told her the night before, about his sister, she didn't have the heart to push him for more. And anyway, maybe she didn't need to. Maybe it was obvious why he'd changed his mind. Maybe, like her, he just wanted to take what they had together, where they could forget about real life for a while.

So she'd agreed. Without hesitation.

The honeymoon, as it turned out, had involved a couple of days where they only left Castor's bedroom in the villa for sustenance. Then when their hunger for each other had been sated, Castor asked her where else she wanted to go.

Glory had no idea. She'd never imagined leaving LA and yet here she was on a private island in Greece, married to a beautiful billionaire. And when Castor suggested Italy, she said yes, because why not Italy?

She'd sent Annabel another email telling her that everything was okay and that she'd decided to extend her vacation by another couple of weeks. She'd half expected her sister to have seen the news about her marriage to Castor since the news sites were full of it, but Annabel had never taken much notice of celebrity gossip and her response, when it came, was only to hope Glory had a good time and to take care with her money.

Their first port of call had been Rome and since she didn't have any idea what she wanted to do, he'd organised various private tours of the city including the galleries, the ancient sites and the shopping districts. Glory loved all of it. Just being in a different country and especially one as old as Italy was the most wonderful experience.

She discovered she loved history, the ancient sites in particular holding a fascination for her, so much so that Castor organised for a historian to come on one of the tours with them.

At first Glory had worried that Castor might not enjoy this as much as she did, because surely all of this had to be old hat for him. But he gave no sign of being bored. He seemed to enjoy the tour with the historian particularly, peppering the man with all kinds of questions, before turning to Glory and asking her what she thought. He was always asking her what she thought, in fact, and he always listened intently when she told him, as if her opinion mattered to him.

It made her feel important and valued, and maybe it was then that she realised she was falling in love with him. Or maybe it was in Venice, when he took her on a gondola ride only to chat to the gondolier for half an hour, somehow getting the man from only answering questions in monosyllables, to a full-blown soliloquy about his beautiful wife and his lovely children, and how he worried sometimes that he didn't earn enough to care for them. As they left the gondola, without a word Castor gave the man a tip that left him speechless and made Glory's heart squeeze tight.

Or maybe it was in Milan, where he gave her a Cinderella moment in an exclusive designer's salon, having her try on gown after gown, and telling her how beautiful she looked in all of them. Before buying them all, much to Glory's shock, because she was never going to wear them. She told him so and he nodded seriously, then turned around and donated all but Glory's favourite to a charity who could sell the gowns off to make money for disadvantaged kids.

He was a good man. A very good man. Kind and thoughtful and generous. He was excellent company with a dry wit that she very much enjoyed, and even though he was quite serious, she found that she had the ability to make him smile after all. Rare, genuine smiles that she treasured like the gifts they were.

Really, Glory thought now as she looked at herself in the gown she'd chosen in Milan, it wasn't any wonder if she was falling for him, because what woman wouldn't? Especially when he was so irresistible.

She'd tried not to. Tried to tell herself that was a stupid thing to do, because there was no future for them, he'd been very clear about that. She might be married to him, but their marriage wasn't real. And this honeymoon would be over in a couple of weeks, and then she'd go on with her life.

A life without him in it.

But she didn't want to think about that, so she didn't, preferring to live in the moments they had together and not wishing for something that couldn't ever be. After all, he'd never promised her anything more and she didn't have the right to ask for it. He had his own burdens to bear and she couldn't add to them by demanding something from him that he wasn't going to give.

How could he? When it was clear that what had happened to his sister ruled his life? She'd thought it would be something terrible and indeed it was, just as it was obvious that he blamed himself. He hadn't said so explicitly, but she'd seen the pain glittering deep in his eyes. She understood what it was to feel responsible for another's hurt.

That night she'd sensed he didn't want to talk about it so she hadn't pushed him, merely given him what distraction she could. But the look on his face haunted her, made her want to know more. For example, was this mission of his an atonement? Or was it a punishment? Or was it perhaps both?

Whatever it was, she couldn't get it out of her head and she wanted to help him. But she didn't know how.

You couldn't help Annabel. What makes you think you can help him?

The thought was a cold one, so she pushed it away.

Tonight he'd planned another Cinderella moment for her, a ball, and so she wanted to enjoy it, not depress herself with doubts.

The gown she wore tonight was of gold silk, wrapping around her body like the kind of gown a Grecian goddess would wear, and it fitted perfectly. A stylist had come to do her hair and make-up, which she loved, because it made her feel like a princess and she'd had so few princess moments in her life that she couldn't help but enjoy it.

Castor had told her that he was going to wait downstairs for her and to take her time coming down, because he wanted to see her make a grand entrance.

Glory had never made a grand entrance to anything and she was a little nervous as she came to the sweeping marble staircase that led down to the mansion's entranceway.

Castor stood by the front door waiting for her, dressed in plain, unadorned black evening wear, nothing to compete with the astonishing beauty of his face. The stark colour highlighted the golden strands in his dark tawny hair and drew attention to the smoky amber of his eyes. He looked like a god out of Greek myth and she felt the oddest sense of dislocation, because how could a man like that be waiting for her?

How could you have all these nice things when Annabel, who had to give up so much for you, gets nothing?

No, she couldn't think those things, and besides,

that's why she was here, wasn't it? So Annabel could get the one thing she'd always wanted.

These doubts were ridiculous, and she wasn't going to think about them any more.

Putting one hand on the banister, Glory moved slowly down the stairs to where Castor waited.

'I was right,' he murmured, the look in his eyes catching fire. 'You have the most appropriate name. Glory, you are glorious.'

She flushed, inordinately pleased with herself and not a little pleased with him too. 'So are you,' she said, coming to a stop in front of him. 'Glorious, I mean.'

She expected him to smile, but he didn't. Instead the fierce gleam in his gaze only seemed to burn hotter. It was familiar that look. As if he was a dragon and she was the treasure he guarded.

Not that she was *his* treasure. She was only a woman he'd signed a contract with to marry and whom he was currently sleeping with, so why he'd even look at her that way was anyone's guess.

What was worse, however, was that part of her liked how fiercely he looked at her, as if there was nothing more important in his world than she was. Part of her wanted it, and because she was going to have this moment, this night, and not worry about real life, she said nothing, taking his hand when he held it out to her and letting him lead her outside.

A limo waited in the street for them and Glory was too busy looking at that to notice there were rather more men in plain dark suits standing around than there usually were.

She'd spotted them first in Italy and had asked Castor about what they were doing. He'd shrugged as if it was no big deal, telling her it was his security team, and that he always had security with him whenever he was out in public.

She'd accepted this since it made sense, given the facade he projected and the people he associated with, and since the security team was discreet, she soon forgot about it.

But as she'd finished marvelling at the limo and prepared to get in, she realised that there were twice as many security staff as there normally were.

'There are a lot of men in suits standing around tonight,' she said, after Castor had got into the limo beside her and they'd pulled away into the traffic. 'Did you hire more security staff?'

'Just a few more.' He took her hand, warm strong fingers enfolding hers. 'Tell me, would you object if I decided to ravish you in the back of this limo?'

That he was distracting her, she understood, but since she wasn't sure why, she decided to let him, dismissing the issue of security for now.

The gala was being held at the Musée d'Orsay and she wasn't surprised to find a contingent of press outside the doors.

They'd been followed around Europe by a press pack and while she hadn't quite got used to it, she was at least less anxious about being photographed than she'd been the day they left LA.

Castor had helped, carefully orchestrating their photo opportunities so she was comfortable and so that it didn't feel like too much of an intrusion, and he did so now, taking her hand once again, the warmth of his touch steadying her. But he didn't speak as he drew her out of the limo. He didn't look at her either, his attention on the gathered press, his expression oddly grim.

Drawing her close to his side, he hurried her inside despite the pleas for a photo opportunity and questions shouted at him from the waiting media.

It puzzled her, as did the hard expression on his face. Other people were arriving, dressed in beautiful gowns and suits, a crowd beginning to build, and he kept scanning them as if looking for someone.

'Castor,' Glory murmured, as he hurried her down an echoing, white and gilt corridor to where the gala was being held. 'Is everything okay?'

He didn't stop, but his expression was hard. 'It's fine. Why do you ask?'

'You keep looking around like you're trying to find someone.'

'Just checking security.' His fingers tightened around hers. 'Come, the party is this way.'

Glory frowned. He was radiating tension and was clearly not fine, but there were people all around and this was not either the time or the place for that discussion, so all she did was nod and let him lead her into the gallery where the gala was being held.

It was all high, domed ceilings, gilded columns and vast chandeliers. Trees in tubs stood at intervals, the trunks and branches wound around with fairy lights, and at one end a woman in a long gown played a gilded harp, flooding the air with delicate music.

Crowds of people ebbed and flowed around the gallery, the women in beautiful gowns, the men in exquisitely tailored evening wear, while wait staff circulated with drinks.

Glory was sure she'd spotted several A-list actors in the crowds, as well as a politician or two. It felt like being in a dream.

Castor's grip on her hand tightened and she found herself pulled very firmly up against him. His arm slid possessively around her waist, his fingers spreading out on her hip.

She liked being held against him like this, it made her feel treasured, but that strange tension that gathered around him wasn't going away. She could feel it in the arm around her, in the hand that pressed into her hip, in the hot, hard torso she was being held against.

People were turning their heads in their direction, whispering and pointing. The tension in Castor's arm increased. Yet when he moved it was with that natural ease and grace she'd come to associate with him, the mask he wore, his charming smile, firmly in place.

It had been so long since she'd seen it she'd almost forgotten the persona he wore around other people. She didn't like it, she realised. She didn't like him having to hide himself, to pretend to be this other jaded, dissolute man, and she didn't like others thinking he was that same man too.

Because he wasn't. He was so many other wonderful things and she hated, all of a sudden, that he hid his true self away.

He has to do that, remember? He's playing a part.

Yes, his mission to take down those trafficking rings by infiltrating them. By turning himself into one of those men. And he'd been doing it for at least a decade…

A sudden grief constricted around her heart as Castor guided them around the gallery, greeting people, answering questions and receiving congratulations on their marriage.

She glanced up at him, the discomfort she'd had coming in deepening. His handsome features had become hard, almost cold, his gaze relentlessly scanning the room. She noticed the black-suited men moving through the room too, fanning out around her and Castor like a protective shield.

He'd been living like this for a long time, pretending to be someone else, pretending to be as awful as the people he associated with. And that had to have affected him. If there was one thing she'd learned about him in the past two weeks, it was that he was a protective, caring man and capable of great kindness. What had all this pretence done to him? Was he tired of it? Did he want to lay down the burden of having to do this just once?

If he was anything like Annabel and how she'd felt while caring for Glory, then yes, he probably did.

Because that's why he was doing this, wasn't it? It was for his sister's sake.

The constriction of grief tightened inside her. It wasn't fair that had happened to him. And it was clear the night he'd told her what happened that he blamed himself for it and had been spending the last twenty years of his life trying to make up for it. Why else would he be driven?

She wanted to help him, but she didn't know how. He had a right to his feelings and she wasn't anything to him but one of his lovers. Who was she to try to give him comfort? When she hadn't even been able to comfort her own sister?

Still, she could perhaps try, in her own small way.

'Castor,' she murmured as they threaded their way through the crowds. 'It's okay. I'm not going to disappear or anything.'

He glanced down at her, his gaze narrowing into smoky amber slits. The charming man he'd been just seconds before vanishing and leaving behind a dangerous-looking stranger. 'What are you talking about?'

As she'd told herself a number of times tonight already, an exclusive gala wasn't the place for such a discussion. But she couldn't stay silent. He was alone in this, she knew that. He'd told no one else, which made her the only one here who could offer any help. She couldn't turn away from him, no matter how little confidence she had in her ability to comfort him.

'You,' she said quietly. 'You're incredibly tense and you haven't let me go all evening.'

He looked away, giving the room another survey, his grip on her hand tightening. 'This place isn't safe for you.'

'Why not?'

'I had word that some of the guests here are part of that Eastern European trafficking ring.' He scanned over the crowds yet again. 'They wanted to see my bride for themselves, which means I have to protect you.'

Glory knew that should frighten her, but it didn't. What frightened her more was the tension in him. 'I'm okay.' She squeezed his hand. 'You don't have to—'

Very suddenly, before she could say a word, he pulled her aside into the shadow of a gilded column, out of the way of the rest of the crowd. Then with firm hands he pushed her up against a wall and caged her there with his body, his palms on either side of her head as he looked down at her, his gaze blazing.

'Don't question me,' he said in a low, rough voice. 'You're *my* wife. I am responsible for your care and protection, and I will do it as I see fit.'

The ferocity in his voice shocked her as did the burning look in his eyes. He was staring at her as if he was furious with her, looming over her, his powerful body keeping her caged. And if she hadn't known him, hadn't known about his sister, she would have been frightened.

But she did know him and she wasn't scared. Because he wasn't angry. He was afraid for her. He was trying to protect her.

It's not about you, come on. He's still trying to save his sister even after all those years.

Her heart ached with a complicated kind of pain. Pain for the grief that still had a hold on him. Pain for how hard he drove himself. And pain for herself, that it wasn't her specifically he was afraid for, because deep down, she wanted it to be.

But what a selfish thought that was. This man had too many burdens to bear already, he didn't need her adding to them. What she should be doing was lightening the load.

So she reached up and cupped his hard jaw, trying to reassure him. 'It's okay. We can go home if you like. If that's easier for you.'

The expression on his face didn't change, his fierce gaze burning into hers for one long, unaccountable second.

Then he leaned forward and took her mouth.

Castor knew this wasn't the place for such displays—not that he'd ever let it bother him in the past—but he couldn't stop himself.

Her hand was on his jaw, her touch a sweet relief, and she smelled so warm and sexy and familiar. And right here, in the circle of his arms, no one could touch her, no one could hurt her. She was completely his. The dread that had gripped him the moment he'd had word that people from the Eastern European ring were here to take a look at Glory themselves.

Three weeks ago, it wouldn't have concerned him. He knew his security was faultless and that she would be safe. But that was before he'd spent two weeks with her in his bed, holding her. Two weeks of her smile and her wonder and her simple joy at all the new things he'd introduced her to. Two weeks of taking care of someone and watching how it made a difference to them directly, instead of wondering if anything he did helped anyone. Because no matter how many people he helped, there were always more.

She gave him hope, that was the problem. For the first time in years, the weight he carried felt lighter when she was around, and that was dangerous. Because eventually he'd have to pick it back up again and he had to be strong when he did so. He couldn't afford any weakness, any chink in his armour.

He'd thought he was fine though. The gala appearance was to solidify Glory's presence as his wife, and his contact had already told him to expect an invitation from one of shadowy heads of the trafficking ring, which meant his ruse was working.

But what he hadn't expected was the dread that had gripped him the moment they'd stepped out of the limo. The dread that centred on Glory and something happening to her. Something he couldn't prevent or save her from.

He'd tried to brush it off, tried to ignore the cold fear the way he'd been ignoring all his emotions for the past twenty years. But it didn't work. And the longer the night went on, the more the dread tightened its grip until he could hardly breathe.

He had to ground himself somehow and her kiss

was what he needed, her warmth and her touch, to keep that dread at bay.

You know why you're so afraid. You feel something for her.

Castor kissed her deeper, harder, fighting the truth. The truth he'd tried for the past two weeks to ignore, that made him feel like a man sinking into the ocean, and dragged down to the bottom, unable to get free.

He'd thought her so ordinary that she wouldn't be in any danger, that she'd be instantly forgotten, a nameless, faceless woman he could divorce in a year or so and no one would ever even be interested.

But he was wrong, as he'd been wrong about so many things. She wasn't ordinary, not in any way, and if he could see that, then so could others.

They could threaten her. They could take her from him. They could make her disappear like Ismena had disappeared, and if that happened a second time, he knew he wouldn't survive it.

Then you know what you have to do, don't you?

Oh, he did. And he'd have given anything not to feel this, not to care, but it was already too late for him. There was only one way out.

But first, he could have this.

Her mouth was soft under his and so very hot, her hands lifting to cup his face, and suddenly the most intense desperation filled him.

He pushed her harder against the wall, wanting her taste in his mouth, her soft curves against his body, her scent everywhere. Because there was only one way to save her and he just didn't want to do it. Not yet.

Castor broke the kiss, his breathing harsh in the small space between them. 'I need you, Glory,' he said roughly. 'Now.'

Her eyes were very wide, her face flushed. 'Here? But…'

He shoved himself away from the wall and took a quick look around, but it seemed as if no one had seen them. Good.

Without a word, he took her hand in his, headed to one of the exits and down an echoing corridor. A door stood slightly ajar and so he pulled her into the room beyond it, shutting the door hard behind them and locking it for good measure.

It turned out to be an office of some kind, not that he cared.

Taking Glory by the hips, he pushed her gently up against the wall and bent once more, brushing his mouth against her. '*Mikri alepou*, will you let me have you? I have to… I need…' His breathing was getting out of control, the desperation winding in a tight band around his chest. Just once more to have her in his arms, once more to be inside her. Once more to hold her against his heart.

'Please, Glory…'

She was frowning up at him, concern in her eyes. 'What's going on?' Her hands were pressed to his chest and she was smoothing the cotton of his shirt absently as if trying to soothe him. 'You're upset.'

It felt like someone had grabbed his heart in their

hands and were slowly squeezing it tight, and he didn't know what to do. He should talk to her, explain himself, but right now there was only one thing he could think of that would help.

He kissed her again, feeling her stiffen slightly, then relax against him, her hands spreading wide on his chest, then moving up to his shoulders, creeping around his neck.

Theos, she was such a gift.

This is the last time.

It would have to be. He couldn't put her in this danger, where associating with him would draw the wrong attention. And he couldn't allow her to get any closer to him than she already was. That integrity of his emotional detachment was under threat and he couldn't permit it to be weakened any further.

He should never have taken her on a honeymoon, never have spent the past two weeks with her. He should have walked away after their wedding and never seen her again.

The hand around his heart squeezed hard, making pain radiate throughout his entire body, but he ignored it.

Time to think about that later, now he just needed her.

Gently, he pulled her arms from around his neck, before dropping to his knees at her feet. Then he reached beneath the hem of her magnificent gown, his palms sliding behind her calves before moving higher, her skin smooth and warm and silky, drawing the hem of her gown up with it.

She trembled slightly, but he could hear the uneven sound of her breath, could see the look in her eyes as she stared down at him. There was heat in the deep brown of her gaze, the strong flame of the passion she kept hidden behind her sharp little face.

A passion that set him on fire.

He leaned in as he slid his hands up the backs of her thighs, stroking her and making her shake, then he touched the lacy front of her panties, stroking the soft heat of her until the fabric became damp and the scent of her arousal filled his senses.

He held her gaze as he pulled aside the fabric before covering her with his mouth, tasting her. She jerked in his grip, letting out a gasp, her hands coming to his shoulders and holding on for dear life. Her gaze turned dark and even smokier than it already was, her cheeks turning a deep rose.

Beautiful little fox.

He took her to the edge of pleasure and then tipped her over it, the taste of her sweet and musky in his mouth, her cries loud in his ears. Then as she was still trembling through the aftershocks, he rose to his feet and pushed her against the wall. He undid his fly, slid one hand beneath her thigh and hauled it up around his waist, dealt with the protection, positioned himself and thrust hard into her hot, slick sex.

She cried out, her hips lifting against his, clutching at him as he moved, hard and deep and fast, losing himself in the sweet grip of her body around his sex, in the sounds she made, in the scent of her everywhere around him.

Her like this would be a memory he would treasure for ever.

He wanted to make it last, wanted for this to be something she'd remember for ever too, but he was too desperate, and in the end he had to slip a hand between her thighs, stroking her until the sound of her climax echoed in his ears.

And then he followed her, losing himself in the dizzying rush of pleasure for just a few moments.

Yet real life was always going to intrude and it intruded now, rushing back on him, weighing him down, crushing him.

He didn't want to make this choice, but he had to. The only way he could continue his mission effectively was to detach himself fully from the intensity of his own emotions. And he couldn't do that with Glory around.

He would have to end this and quickly.

CHAPTER TEN

GLORY WAS BARELY aware of anything as Castor smoothed her gown over her shaking thighs, then adjusted his own clothing. Her heart was beating far too fast and the throb between her legs was an aching reminder of what had just happened between them.

Without a word, he took her hand and led them out of the room, moving fast down the corridor and out of the gallery.

She found the lights blinding, still processing the stunning effects of the orgasm he'd given her as he pulled her down the steps. His hand was strong and warm in hers, and it was a good thing he knew what he was doing, because she was still dazed.

The limo was waiting for them and soon they were both inside and pulling away into the late-night Parisian traffic. And it was only then that Glory began to process what was going on, because something was.

First he'd kissed her like he was desperate, and then he'd pushed her into an empty room. And when she'd asked him what was going on, he hadn't answered her. Only made love to her as if his life depended on it.

She didn't understand.

'Castor?' Her voice sounded a bit rough and scratchy. 'What's wrong?'

He was sitting opposite her in the limo, his elbows on his knees, his hands clasped. His attention was on the floor, the expression on his beautiful face shuttered.

He was silent for a long moment, then without looking up he said, 'I have to return to the States tomorrow. Some pressing work issues have come up.'

Her stomach lurched with a disappointment she tried to tell herself she didn't feel, because of course their time together had always been limited. This couldn't go on for ever. 'Okay. So are you going to tell me—?'

'You can stay in France as long as you wish. My staff will be at your complete disposal.'

She stared at his shuttered face. He'd been so desperate back there in that room, holding onto her tightly, as if he'd been afraid she'd slip away from him.

Or as if that was the last time…

A thread of ice wound through her. She didn't want to ask, but she had to know.

'Is this it?' Her voice sounded hoarse. 'Is this the end? Is this goodbye?'

He lifted his head, his amber gaze gone suddenly cold, as if there was a sheet of glass between them. 'Give some thought as to where you want to live as my wife. I'll have my property manager give you a list of suitable properties. There's a place in the Hollywood Hills you might like. Or if you'd prefer the east coast, I have a penthouse in New York that will suit.'

Yes, apparently so. This was goodbye.

Her eyes prickled, her throat closing.

You always knew that this wasn't real, that it was only temporary.

Yes, and she'd told herself so many times these past two weeks. But all of that hadn't helped her prepare for the moment when it would all end. And now that moment was here it was every bit as painful and terrible as she thought it would be.

Why are you so upset?

Oh, she knew why. She knew down to her soul. She wasn't falling for Castor Xenakis, she'd already fallen, hard and fast and irrevocably.

She was in love with him and she didn't know what to do about it.

'We can't...we can't have another week?' she asked, hating how desperate she sounded, yet unable to stop herself from asking.

Castor's gaze flickered, then he shook his head slowly. 'No, *mikri alepou*, I'm afraid that will not be happening.' Slowly, he sat up, his gaze unwavering. 'You're right though. This is where we part ways.'

She didn't want to be needy, didn't want to demand things of him that he couldn't give her, because as she'd told herself time and time again, she didn't have the right.

Yet she couldn't stop the words from coming out. 'What about another few days? Surely that's okay?'

'That will only be putting off the inevitable.' He let out a breath. 'This was never going to be real, Glory, I told you that. And it can't be, understand?'

She swallowed, her throat suddenly thick. 'Why not? Why can't it be real?'

The cold mask that had settled over his features rippled, revealing what lay underneath, that bleak expression and a rawness that made her chest feel like it was full of broken glass.

'Because I can't,' he said, suddenly fierce. 'Because it's too dangerous for you, and now that you're my wife, you'll be put in harm's way.'

'But I'm already in harm's way,' she said a little desperately. 'And you have a lot of security. And I don't mind—'

'You might not, but I do.' His gaze burned as he stared at her. '*I* can't do it, Glory. *I* can't let anything happen to you. You're too important to me already and you shouldn't be. You're a threat to my mission and I can't allow that to continue.'

Shock stole her breath. 'A threat? What are you talking about?'

His expression shifted for a moment, became softer, warmer. '*Mikri alepou*, you have no idea what the past two weeks have meant and how much I've enjoyed being with you. It was a…respite for me. Some time out from reality and I needed it. But I have a mission to get back to and I can't be effective if I'm worrying about someone. If I'm afraid for someone.'

She understood. She understood all too well. She was a burden to him, an obstacle preventing him from doing what he needed to do, the way she'd been with Annabel.

Seriously? So that's it? You're not even going to protest?

But how could she protest? How could she demand that he consider her feelings? He was trying to save people and she wasn't more important than all of them. She wasn't more important to his mission.

'I...get it,' she said huskily, her chest aching. 'I really do. I wouldn't want to get in the way of what you're doing.'

The warmth drained slowly from his expression, the lines of his face hardening once again. 'I have to do this, Glory. You understand that, don't you?'

She wasn't sure why he seemed to think she was arguing with him. 'Of course I understand.'

'It's for Ismena's sake.' Gold glittered in his eyes. 'It was my fault that night. I was the one who took her out and all because I wanted to talk to some girl. Because I put my own needs first.' A muscle jumped in the side of his jaw. 'I shouldn't have. I should have been watching out for her. I should have protected her. And I didn't.'

The broken glass in Glory's chest shifted around, cutting into her. There was so much pain in his beautiful voice, so much self-recrimination, that she forgot her own hurt, leaning across the space between them and reaching for his hand, taking it in hers.

'Stop punishing yourself, Castor,' she said thickly. 'Please, stop.'

He went still, his gaze flaring. 'Glory...'

'Don't think I can't see it,' she went on, because now the words were out she had to keep going. 'You were fifteen. You were a child. How were you to know what was going to happen? You couldn't have predicted—'

'No.' The word fell like a sword, heavy and edged and lethal. 'You think I can excuse myself simply because I was fifteen? Everyone knew there were traffickers about in our neighbourhood—it was common gossip. Do you think I took any notice? No, I didn't.' He spat out a curse in Greek then, rough and guttural, and ripped his hand from hers. 'I was her older brother and I should have protected her, and there is no forgiveness for my failure. None at all.'

The warmth of his fingers in hers lingered on her skin, but the pain of his withdrawal stung. She didn't know what to say or how to help him, because she'd never suffered a loss like he had, not something so terrible. It was true that she'd lost her parents but that was an old grief, and not one she'd ever blamed herself for the way he had.

You have something to offer him though.

Glory took a breath as realisation came to her. Because yes, she did. She might be a plain, ordinary checkout girl, but there was one thing that she was that he wasn't.

She was someone's little sister.

She braced herself, then met his gaze and held it, blinking back her tears. 'Your sister would forgive you. And she wouldn't want you punishing yourself. It would have broken her heart if she knew you'd spent the last twenty years torturing yourself for something that wasn't even your fault to begin with.'

His eyes blazed with sudden fury. 'What would you know about it? What would you know about what she would and wouldn't have done? Ismena wasn't your sister. She was mine!'

Glory didn't look away. 'What would I know? I know that I would have done anything to make Annabel's life better. Because watching my older sister run herself into the ground trying to take care of me just about broke my heart.' The tears she'd been holding back suddenly spilled out, running down her cheeks, but she didn't stop them. 'And if I was Ismena, that's exactly how I'd feel, watching you suffer for something you shouldn't take the blame for.'

He stared at her for a long moment, the anger dying out of his eyes, leaving behind it that terrible bleakness, that terrible grief. 'I don't know,' he said roughly, 'why you'd even care.'

Glory swallowed. 'Why? Because I'm in love with you.'

He'd thought, that after the last twenty years, he'd got rid of the last remnants of his own heart. But apparently he was wrong, because looking into Glory's eyes, he could feel the remains of it tearing itself apart.

He let it though, let it tear itself to pieces in his chest. Because he didn't want it. Love was another threat to his mission, another weakness he couldn't afford. Love was nothing but recrimination and grief and twenty years of grinding sorrow, and he didn't want anything to do with it.

Even her love?

Castor ignored the thought. There was no point in continuing this conversation and dragging this whole process out. He'd made his decision and it didn't matter if Glory didn't like it, just as it didn't matter what she felt for him.

He'd said goodbye in that room in the Musée d'Orsay, he'd taken his last fill of her, and now it was over.

Why? There is an alternative, you know. Your life doesn't have to be all about the mission.

A ridiculous thought. His life was *only* the mission. His sister demanded justice and he would give it to her somehow. Otherwise what would be the point of the past twenty years?

Castor stared at the warm, lovely woman sitting opposite; she wasn't so ordinary after all, and never had been. He felt…nothing. An echoing coldness in his chest where his heart had once been. It was comforting.

'I'm sorry,' he said flatly. 'That is not my problem.' He turned, hit the button on the intercom. 'Stop the car.'

Glory took a shaken breath. 'Castor…'

The limo came to a stop.

'Castor, please.'

He found himself pulling at his tie, trying to get some air, because it felt as if he could hardly breathe.

Already this whole scene had gone on too long. It was time to bring it to an end.

Ignoring her, Castor opened the door, got out and strode away.

He didn't return to the mansion that night. Instead he took the jet to London, then spent a week at his company's London office, before crossing the Atlantic to New York. His staff informed him that Glory was still in Paris, which was fine. He told them to keep him posted.

Then he got the invite he'd been waiting for to an exclusive party thrown by the inner circle of the group he'd been trying to infiltrate. Apparently rumours of his wedding had been circulating and there had been 'approval' from certain quarters.

He would get his meeting.

Castor told himself he was pleased since obviously marrying her had been a good thing, but no matter the emptiness in the centre of his chest, the dread wouldn't leave him. He put extra men in the security team he still had watching her, already going over plans for how he could take her out of range of the people he was dealing with.

Somehow, he would do it. He was the one who'd put her in danger by dragging her into this mess, and so he would be the one who would protect her.

You hurt her.

Yes, he had. But better the wound to her heart than anything else. Besides, she deserved someone who would put her first, and that someone wasn't him.

His mission was more important and always would be.

Eventually he got word that Glory had returned to LA, but not to any of his residences. She'd gone back to her apartment, which he didn't understand, not when she could have had any property she wanted.

Then again, who was he to argue? He'd let her go. He'd put distance between them, and that distance would have to stay. He made sure his security team was keeping an eye on her though, not that it mattered any more.

Not now he'd finally stopped caring.

CHAPTER ELEVEN

GLORY SAT AT the kitchen table in the run-down apartment she shared with Annabel and waited.

The flight from Paris had taken it out of her, and not only was she heartbroken, she was also jet-lagged and exhausted, and the very last thing she felt like doing was fronting up to Annabel with the truth.

But she couldn't bear the thought of lying any longer.

She couldn't bear the thought of pretending either.

She'd tried to do that in Paris the whole past week, telling herself her heart wasn't broken in two, and that she didn't ache for him, or miss him, or wish he was with her every second of the day. And of course that hadn't worked. Being in his mansion, surrounded by the memories of the precious couple of weeks they'd had together, only made the pain in her heart more acute.

So she'd finally packed her bags and headed home, taking with her the knowledge that the only thing she had left was the truth.

She loved him, but he didn't love her. He'd walked away.

A part of her had wanted to go after him when he'd got out of the limo, to demand they discuss it, but it had taken all she had simply to tell him the truth and she hadn't had the strength to face him. Not when it was so obvious that her love was just another burden he had to bear.

Sure, keep telling yourself it's all about not having the right to push him or not wanting to be a burden, when the truth is you're just terrified you're not good enough for him.

She wasn't sure what to think about that, but then she heard the key in the lock of the front door and a couple of minutes later Annabel came into the kitchen.

Her sister's brown eyes widened and she stopped dead in the doorway. 'Glory? You're back!'

Glory sucked in a breath. 'Hi, Anna,' she said thickly. 'I…need to talk to you.'

'Where have you been?' Annabel demanded, taking a couple of steps into the room, her shock moving into anger. 'I've been worried sick—'

'I lied to you,' Glory interrupted, needing to get this over and done with as quickly as possible. 'I'm sure you know that already. I'm sure you've seen the news.'

'Lied to me about what? And no, I haven't seen anything on the news.'

Glory sighed. 'You haven't seen the news about me and Castor Xenakis?'

'That billionaire guy?' Her sister frowned. 'What about him? What's he got to do with this? And what have you been doing?'

So, Glory explained everything that had happened, starting with that night in Castor's mansion and detailing the wedding, the honeymoon and finally the gala in Paris and how he'd left her. The only thing she left out was his mission since that wasn't her secret to give.

When she was done, Annabel looked at her in dumbfounded silence, and just like that Glory decided she was done with avoiding confrontation and making things okay for her sister.

She'd been letting Annabel's opinion guide her life for far too long and she was over it. Just as she was over pretending she wasn't in love with a man out of her league and unsuitable for her in every way.

'Just so you know,' Glory said into the tense silence, 'I don't care if you're disappointed in me. And if you don't want to pursue the IVF because Castor paid for it, then that's up to you.' She drew herself up, finding inside her the same well of strength she'd discovered with Castor. 'But you should know that I don't regret marrying him and I don't regret spending two weeks with him in Europe. And most of all, I don't regret loving him, because I do.'

For a long moment there was silence and then Annabel sighed. 'I wasn't the best sister to you, was I?'

Glory blinked, not expecting this. 'What? Of course you were. You were the best. I couldn't have asked—'

'Because if I was,' Annabel went on as if Glory hadn't spoken. 'You would have told me the truth. You wouldn't have felt you had to lie.'

Glory stared at her. Because it wasn't an accusation. It sounded more like…regret. And it was on the tip of her tongue to tell Annabel that she'd lied to save her worry, but that would be doing both of them a disservice.

She wasn't a child any more. She wasn't the little sister Annabel had to look after. She was an adult and she could handle the truth. If anything, Castor had shown her that.

'I'm sorry I lied,' Glory said at last. 'I didn't want you to talk me out of it and I…didn't want to be treated like a child. As if I can't be trusted to make my own decisions.'

Annabel shook her head. 'Oh, Glor… I never meant… It wasn't…' She trailed off. 'All I wanted to do—all I *ever* wanted to do—was protect you. You understand that, don't you?'

'I do,' Glory said. 'And all I ever wanted to do was to save you from worry.'

For a long moment the two of them looked at each other. Then Annabel crossed the kitchen and wrapped her arms around Glory, giving her a giant hug. 'I'm so sorry he left,' she murmured as Glory hugged her back. 'For what it's worth, he's an idiot to walk away.'

A tension Glory hadn't even known she was feeling gradually ebbed. 'He had his reasons.'

Annabel released her, then stepped back. 'Why didn't you go after him?'

Glory sighed. 'I…couldn't.'

'Why not?' And then suddenly something fierce glowed in her sister's gaze. 'You love him, don't you?'

Glory swallowed. 'Well, yes…'

You know why you didn't go after him.

Oh, she did. And it wasn't so much a realisation as an admission.

She'd let him go. She hadn't stopped him from getting out of the limo and she hadn't gone after him the next day. She hadn't made any attempt to contact him afterwards; she'd simply drifted around Paris in a devastated fashion trying to pull herself together enough to get home.

And now she was home. Back in her old apartment, ready to resume her old life. Was that all there was? Was that what she was doomed to? Watching her sister finally get what she wanted, while she sat behind the counter with no dreams and no plans. Never allowing herself to think of all the things *she* wanted.

Because you never thought you deserved them. Because you never thought you were good enough for them.

It was true. And as Glory stared sightlessly at her sister, all she could think about was the time she'd had with Castor and all the things he'd showed her, the big wide world outside her narrow LA existence.

A world she'd never thought would be within reach of a girl like her.

Yet she'd not only reached for it, she'd held it in her hands.

A world with Castor in it.

A world where she was good enough for him.

Glory took a ragged breath, pain curling around her heart. Pain because she hadn't held on to that world, she'd let it go. She'd been afraid and hurt, and so it was easier to open her fingers and release it, than to stay and fight for it.

Like Annabel had stayed and fought for her, even when things had been hard.

Like Castor had fought for his sister too, even through his grief.

Because that was love, wasn't it? It wasn't turning tail and running when things got hard; it was digging in and staying despite it.

Because it was worth it.

He was worth it.

Something rippled through her, a powerful wave of emotion, the same kind of emotion that had propelled her into Castor's mansion that first night a couple of months earlier.

She couldn't stay here, safe in her little world. She had to find the courage of her own convictions. She had to fight for the world she wanted, a world with Castor Xenakis in it, and she couldn't let him push her away.

She'd never ask him to give up his mission, never ask him to put her before his sister, but she needed him to know she was there. And she'd be there for him whenever he wanted her, and if he never did, then that was fine too.

He just needed to know that he wasn't alone.

'I...think I've changed my mind,' she said hoarsely. 'I think I might have to go after him after all.'

Annabel didn't look surprised, only nodding as if she'd expected Glory to do this all along. 'Of course you do. Well, you helped me get what I wanted. Now let me help you get you what you want.'

So they sat down with the very old laptop of Annabel's and did a few searches. And eventually uncovered a gossip site full of salacious details of his latest exploits. They were all lies—which she told Annabel, even though she suspected Annabel didn't believe her—but in the last paragraph she found what she was looking for, mention of a party that was to be held in New York.

She'd had one meeting with Castor's property manager before she'd decided that living in one of his residences was a mistake, and the apartment in New York had been one of the properties mentioned. She knew where it was.

All she had to do was get there.

'I'll pay for your ticket,' Annabel said, already bringing up the booking website. 'And don't even think about arguing, Glory Albright.'

So Glory didn't, and a couple of days later, she was on the red-eye to JFK. She bought herself a simple dress of red satin that clung to her curves. And over it she put a cloak she'd found in a thrift store, just the way she had that first time.

The party at the Park Avenue penthouse was a nightmare to get into, and she had to let one of his staff know who she was in order to get in, but eventually they let her take the elevator up to the penthouse suite.

It was like the party in Malibu where she'd met him months earlier, thumping music and crowds of people, lots of beautiful women in beautiful dresses and some of them naked. She ignored them all, moving through the crowd unseen, searching for the one man who outshone all of them.

He was nowhere to be found.

Until she finally pushed open the door into a small office and there he was, standing in front of the floor-to-ceiling windows, looking out over the city skyline.

Her heart clenched at the sight of his tall, familiar figure.

He was alone and he felt alone, and in that moment, she felt it too. They were so similar, her alone in the shadows, him alone in the spotlight.

But it didn't have to be that way.

'Castor,' she murmured.

He went utterly still as if he'd been shot, then he turned around sharply, his face full of shock. 'Glory?'

She stepped into the room and shut the door, her heart thundering. 'I need to talk to you,' she said, then flung off the cloak.

* * *

The hollow space in Castor's chest where his heart should be tolled like a bell.

His little fox was here. His *mikri alepou*. And he couldn't seem to catch his breath.

He'd thought it would be easy not to think of her, and over the couple of weeks he'd thought he'd succeeded. Yet sometimes a glimpse of russet hair or a pair of wide, dark eyes would make his heart race and all his muscles tighten.

Then there were the dreams that left him aroused and aching and wanting more. As if unconsciousness was the only time he could let himself have her.

And as she stood there, so real and lovely with her curls hanging down to her waist and her gorgeous figure outlined to perfection in a red satin dress, he knew all at once he was wrong. That it didn't matter how many times he told himself to forget her or that he didn't care about her, she'd somehow found her way into the empty place inside him, the place where his heart should have been.

And he could feel it now, beating hard and fast as he stared at her, a wild rush of adrenaline pumping through him.

She shouldn't be here, not at one of these parties. It was dangerous.

'What are you doing here?' he demanded, resisting the urge to cross the space between them and drag her into his arms. Because he knew if he did that, he'd never let her go. 'I thought I told you that—'

'Give me five minutes,' she interrupted, her voice very level and very determined. 'I need to tell you something.'

His jaw was tight, everything ached. The music from the party was shuddering through the walls and he suddenly hated it with everything in him. She'd given him a taste of something more than the life he'd been living for the past twenty years, something better, and now he'd had that taste, going back to his mission was starting to feel more and more impossible.

He didn't need her here tempting him and weakening his resolve, not when there was still more he had to do.

'What?' he growled.

'It won't take long, I promise.' Without hesitation, she crossed the space between them and came right up to him, her dark eyes shining. 'I'm sorry,' she said softly. 'I'm sorry I told you that I loved you and then let you go.'

He felt something inside him lurch, as if he'd missed a step going up the stairs. 'What?' he asked, not understanding.

Strangely, her mouth curved in a warm, almost tender smile that felt like it set something ablaze inside him. 'I let you go, Castor. I let you walk away from me without a fight. And I...I shouldn't have.'

She still made no sense to him. 'I don't know what you're talking about. You know this can't happen between us. I thought I made myself clear.'

'Oh, you did. Very clear. But I'm sorry, if you

think you're getting rid of me that easily, you're mistaken.' She lifted a hand and touched the side of his face, her fingertips brushing his skin like falling sparks. 'I know what your mission means to you and I would never ask you to give it up. I would never ask you to choose. But I want you to know that the one thing I'm never giving up is loving you.' Her fingertips brushed the line of his jaw, so softly, so gently. 'I let you go, because I was afraid to fight for you, afraid because I thought I wasn't good enough for you. Afraid of being a burden the way I was for Annabel.'

He couldn't move. Her touch held him frozen the way her touch always had. Made his breath catch and the heart he was so sure was dead and gone race.

'But I'm not afraid any more, Castor.' Her gaze was black velvet, soft and deep. 'Love doesn't run away from a fight. It doesn't avoid confrontation. It doesn't break when things get hard either, and it was Annabel who showed me that.' Her fingertips brushed his lower lip. 'And you showed me that too.'

'Me?' His voice didn't even sound like his, so rough and guttural.

'Yes.' Her smile deepened. 'Annabel loved me, that's why she cared for me, even when things were hard, and that's what you're doing too. You loved Ismena. You didn't run away when things were hard, and you didn't break when you couldn't find her. You dug in and stayed strong and continued your mission. For her.'

'Glory—'

Her fingertips gently pressed his mouth, silencing him. 'I'm not here to demand things. I just came here to tell you that if you feel the need to keep walking this path, you won't be walking it alone. You'll always have someone in this world who loves you and who'll always be with you, even if the only way you'll allow them to be is in spirit.'

There were tears in her luminous eyes and as he watched, they spilled over and down her cheeks, but she was still smiling. Smiling at him.

Then she went up on her toes and pressed her mouth to his and before he could stop her, she'd let him go and stepped back, taking her warmth and her bright light with her.

'Goodbye, love,' she said softly.

And then she began to turn and walk away.

And with each step she took, he felt the pain inside him grow.

You will always have her, but she will never have you. Because you won't let her. Coward.

How could he give himself to her though? He'd dedicated his life to his sister and the justice she needed, and that would always come first.

No matter what he wanted.

She was nearly at the door now, her hand reaching for the handle.

'Your sister would forgive you. And she wouldn't want you punishing yourself. It would have broken her heart if she knew you'd spent the last twenty years torturing yourself for something that wasn't even your fault to begin with.'

Glory's voice from that night in the limo rang in his head with an insistence he couldn't avoid.

Perhaps he was punishing himself. And perhaps Ismena wouldn't want that for him, but even so, how would that change anything? That would mean the last twenty years of his life would have been for nothing.

'Glory,' he said hoarsely, not even knowing he was going to speak until the words were out.

She turned, tears still streaming down her cheeks, so beautiful and bright in her red dress. His Red Riding Hood. His little fox.

'I can't stop.' The words were ragged and rough and he didn't understand why he was speaking when the quickest way to end this was to let her leave. 'I can't...forgive myself for that night.'

Her hand dropped from the door handle, her dark eyes full of tears and yet unflinching. 'Ismena would.'

His sister's name pierced him like a sword. 'You can't know that.'

But Glory's expression didn't even flicker. 'Would you forgive her if she was you?'

The question cut through him, because he didn't even have to think. Of course he would.

And the answer must have showed on his face, because then she said, 'Don't you understand, Castor? She loved you. And that's what love is. It's forgiveness.'

Something shifted in his chest, pressing against

the heart he kept telling himself was dead. That heart that was painfully, agonisingly alive after all.

'I can't remember,' he said raggedly. 'I can't remember…what that feels like.'

Glory stepped away from the door, then she held out her hand. 'Come to me,' she said softly. 'Come to me and I'll show you.'

He felt frozen then, on the edge of something immense, the feeling in his heart too big for words. Too big for anything.

And abruptly he was back in his house in Malibu a month earlier, only it had been him holding out his hand to her. Offering to show her what it was like to be close to a man.

It seemed appropriate now that she should be the one holding her hand out to him, offering to show him what love felt like.

Except he had a feeling he already knew.

Love was grief and pain and heartache. Love was Ismena.

But love was also joy and pleasure and contentment. Love was Glory in a red dress. Glory poking interestedly around the Colosseum in Rome. Glory coming down the stairs in a golden gown.

Glory throwing off her cloak and offering him her virginity.

Love was Glory.

And he could not walk away from her.

So he took a step. And then another. And then another. Then her hand was in his and he was pulling her against him, or she was pulling him, he wasn't sure. All he knew was that she was finally where she belonged, safe in his arms.

'I love you, Glory,' he whispered into her hair. 'I love you so much.'

She went still and then melted into him, burying her face against his chest, and for a long moment they stood there together in silence, just being together.

Then Glory looked up and said, 'She would have wanted you to be happy. You know that, don't you?'

And he did. Finally, with Glory against him, he could even feel it. 'Yes. But you'll have to show me how happiness works, *mikri alepou*, because I think I've forgotten that too.'

She smiled, pressing herself against him, her eyes shining. 'Oh, you haven't forgotten, Castor Xenakis. In fact, if you kiss me, I guarantee you'll remember.'

So he kissed her and it turned out she was right, he did remember.

He remembered very well.

EPILOGUE

'STOP LOOKING SO NERVOUS,' Glory murmured. 'You'll be fine.' Then she stretched out her hands for the baby currently in Castor's arms.

Castor gave his son a final kiss on the forehead before he reluctantly handed Lucas over to Glory.

He'd never been nervous in his entire life but he was nervous now.

The helicopter had landed and in another couple of moments she'd be here.

Castor took a moment to ground himself by looking at his wife and son, the joy of which he still couldn't believe was his.

The past year had been a busy one. First, he'd used the information he'd managed to get from the heads of the trafficking ring, passing it onto the authorities, and just in time for them to intercept one of the ring's biggest 'shipments' to date. Not only had the authorities managed to save all of the people trafficked, they'd also taken down the heads of the ring itself, just as Castor had hoped.

The news of their capture was a great source of satisfaction to him as he'd disentangled himself from the rest of the web of traffickers he'd once been part of, letting Castor Xenakis, playboy, fade slowly from public life. He was a family man now. He had no need for anything else.

But that didn't mean he'd stopped his mission. No, it had only changed direction. He and Glory had decided to make all his residences safe houses for women in dangerous situations. Any woman could turn up, no questions asked, and they would be taken care of. It had turned out to be a rousing success.

Then six months after he and Glory had been living together, a miracle happened. He'd received the phone call he'd never thought he'd get from a woman he'd thought had died long ago.

The front door of the villa opened and Glory shifted their son in her arms, before taking Castor's hand. And like it had a year ago, he felt her love and strength flow into him, settling him.

'I love you,' he said softly.

She smiled. 'I love you too.'

Then the door opened and a young woman came in. A young woman he'd last seen as a girl, looking at the kittens in a pet store.

A young woman who'd been lost for twenty years and now was found.

Ismena. And she was home.

All Castor's doubts left him.

'Izzy!' he said.

And opened his arms.

* * * * *

#3993 PENNILESS AND PREGNANT IN PARADISE
Jet-Set Billionaires
by Sharon Kendrick

One extraordinary Balinese night in the arms of guarded billionaire Santiago shakes up Kitty's life forever! She'll confess she's pregnant, but she'll need more than their scorching chemistry to accept his convenient proposal!

#3994 THE ROYAL BABY HE MUST CLAIM
Jet-Set Billionaires
by Jadesola James

When a scandalous night results in a shock baby, Princess Kemi ends up wearing tycoon Luke's ring! She fears she's swapping gilded cages as she struggles to break into his impenetrable heart. But will their Seychelles honeymoon set her free?

#3995 INNOCENT IN THE SICILIAN'S PALAZZO
Jet-Set Billionaires
by Kim Lawrence

Soren Steinsson-Vitale knows Anna Randall is totally off-limits. She's his sworn enemy's granddaughter and he's also her boss. But one kiss promises a wild connection that will lead them straight to his palazzo bedroom!

#3996 REVEALING HER NINE-MONTH SECRET
Jet-Set Billionaires
by Natalie Anderson

After one magical evening ended in disaster, Carrie assumed she'd never see superrich Massimo again. So, a glimpse of him nine months later sends her into labor—with the secret she didn't know she was carrying!

HPCNMRA0222

#3997 CINDERELLA FOR THE MIAMI PLAYBOY
Jet-Set Billionaires
by Dani Collins
Bianca Palmer's world hasn't been the same since going into hiding and becoming a housekeeper. So, she's shocked to discover her boss is Everett Drake—the man she shared a mesmerizing encounter with six months ago! And their attraction is just as untamable...

#3998 THEIR ONE-NIGHT RIO REUNION
Jet-Set Billionaires
by Abby Green
When Ana conveniently wed tycoon Caio, they were clear on the terms: one year to expand his empire and secure her freedom. But as the ink dries on their divorce papers, they're forced together for twenty-four hours...and an unrealized passion threatens to combust!

#3999 SNOWBOUND WITH HIS FORBIDDEN PRINCESS
Jet-Set Billionaires
by Pippa Roscoe
Princess Freya is dreading facing Kjell Bergqvist again. He's nothing like the man who broke her heart eight years ago. But memories of what they once shared enflame new desires when a snowstorm leaves them scandalously, irresistibly stranded...

#4000 RETURN OF THE OUTBACK BILLIONAIRE
Jet-Set Billionaires
by Kelly Hunter
Seven years ago, Judah Blake took the fall for a crime he didn't commit to save Bridie Starr. Now his family's land is in *her* hands, and to reclaim his slice of the Australian outback, he'll claim her!

YOU CAN FIND MORE INFORMATION ON UPCOMING HARLEQUIN TITLES, FREE EXCERPTS AND MORE AT HARLEQUIN.COM.

HPCNMRB0222

She needed him to turn. Would she see those disturbingly green
eyes? Would she see a sensual mouth? If he stepped closer would
she hear a voice that whispered wicked invitation and willful
temptation? All those months ago she'd been so seduced by him
she'd abandoned all caution, all reticence for a single night of
silken ecstasy only to then—

A sharp pain lanced, shocking her back to the present. Winded,
she pressed her hand to her stomach. How the mind could wreak
havoc on the body. The stabbing sensation was a visceral reminder
of the desolate emptiness she'd been trying to ignore for so long.

She'd recovered from that heartbreak. She was living her best
life here—free and adventurous, bathing in the warm, brilliant
waters of the Pacific. Her confusion was because she was tired.
But she couldn't resist stepping closer—even as another sharp pain
stole her breath.

"That's interesting." He addressed the man beside him. "Why
are—"

Shock deadened her senses, muting both him and the pain still
squeezing her to the point where she couldn't breathe. That *voice*?
That low tone that invited such confidence and tempted the listener
to share their deepest secrets?

Massimo hadn't just spoken to her. He'd offered the sort of attention that simply stupefied her mind and left her able only to say *yes*. And she had. Like all the women who'd come before her. And doubtless all those after.

Now his brief laugh was deep and infectious. Despite her distance, it was as if he had his head intimately close to hers, his arm around her waist, his lips brushing her highly sensitized skin—

Pain tore through her muscles, forcing her to the present again. She gasped as it seared from her insides and radiated out with increasingly harsh intensity. She stared, helpless to the power of it as that dark head turned in her direction. His green-eyed gaze arrowed on her.

Massimo.

"Carrie?" Sereana materialized, blocking him from her view. "Are you okay?" Her boss looked as alarmed as she sounded.

Carrie crumpled as the cramp intensified. It was as if she'd been grabbed by a ginormous shark and he was trying to tear her in two. "Maybe I ate something…"

Her vision tunneled as she tumbled to the ground.

"Carrie?"

Not Sereana.

She opened her eyes and stared straight into his. "Massimo?"

It couldn't really be him. She was hallucinating, surely. But she felt strong arms close about her. She felt herself lifted and pressed to his broad, hard chest. He was hot and she could hear the thud of his racing heart. Or maybe it was only her own.

If this were just a dream? Fine. She closed her eyes and kept them closed. She would sleep and this awful agony would stop. She really needed it to stop.

"Carrie!"

Don't miss
Revealing Her Nine-Month Secret,
available April 2022 wherever
Harlequin Presents books and ebooks are sold.

Harlequin.com